RENEGADE

CHANTAL FERNANDO

carina press™

carina press™

Recycling programs
for this product may
not exist in your area.

ISBN-13: 978-1-335-21587-1

Renegade

Copyright © 2019 by Chantal Fernando

www.CarinaPress.com

Printed in U.S.A.

Happy thirteenth birthday to my firstborn son.
You are *so* loved.

Author Note

Please note: This book is part of a series but can be read as a standalone.

RENEGADE

Chapter One

"You have got to be kidding me," I groan, slamming my hands down on the steering wheel in frustration. After a week of nothing but bad luck, from locking myself out of my house to smashing the screen on my phone, I shouldn't be surprised that my car has decided to die on me just as I'm about to leave for a road trip to visit my nine-months-pregnant sister, but I am.

After getting out of the car and opening the hood, pretending like I know what I'm supposed to be looking for, I realize that I don't.

Shit.

My car is old, but it's been reliable up until now, and I'm pissed this is the moment it has chosen to be disloyal. I'm going to have to call a mechanic and hope that it can be fixed right now, or I'm screwed.

I type *cheap local mechanics* into my phone when I hear the familiar sound of a motorcycle rumble, a sound I've gotten so used to that it is just background noise. I've been living near the Knights of Fury Motorcycle Club for a few years now, and even though there's a block of vacant land between us, I still call them my neighbors.

My mother and sister told me I was crazy for knowingly moving next to a bunch of bikers, but my house was such a good price, I couldn't turn it down. I suppose I have them to thank for that, because no one else wanted to live near them. Besides, what really is a motorcycle club? I suspect it sounds a lot more nefarious than it really is.

And it hasn't been all bad. Our interactions have been limited to the casual head nod as they ride by. There was one moment where a woman was in a pickle and dropped in to use my phone. There's been no crime in the area, and I surprisingly feel pretty safe.

I start dialing a mechanic and the rumble gets louder as a black Harley comes to a stop behind my car. It's kind of been our unspoken rule that the bikers and I live harmoniously, but don't really engage, so it surprises me when someone gets off the bike and removes his helmet.

Hello, Mr. Biker. He's one good-looking biker, that's for sure. Dark hair, dark eyes, stubble and a tall, built body dressed in all black. He slowly approaches, eyes on my car.

"Need some help?" he says, his deep timbre sending a shiver down my spine.

"That would be great." I'm desperate at this point, especially when the phone rings with no answer from mechanic number one. "I don't know what happened. It only made it down the road before it just stopped."

He comes to stand next to me, and fiddles with the engine before getting in the car and trying to start it to no avail. "I'm going to have to take it in to the clubhouse," he says, frowning. "We can fix it and get it back to you ASAP."

"I appreciate the offer," I say, shifting on my feet as he stares at me. "But I'm kind of supposed to be in Vegas today."

I'm going to have to call the last person I want to call to ask if I can borrow his car.

My father.

Ugh.

"Vegas? We're actually heading that way ourselves. We can give you a ride, if you want," he says, shrugging. "I'm Renny, by the way." He holds out his hand for me to shake.

Renny?

I vaguely remember hearing this name before. Maybe it was when that woman used my phone.

"Isabella," I reply, shaking the tattooed hand. It's big, yet warm and soft, despite the calluses on it.

"I know who you are," he murmurs. "You helped Skylar when she needed it." Skylar, that was her name! "Now why don't you let us return the favor? It's the least we can do."

"I didn't really do anything," I say, surprised he remembers something so small. I mean I let her inside to use my phone, and that's about it. Anyone would do that for someone that they see is visibly in distress.

"You helped. That day..." He pauses with a far-off look on his face. "It was a tough day. We lost someone important and you helping her... Well, it meant a lot. So thank you."

"You're welcome," I say, knowing that arguing would be pointless. "What are neighbors for, right?"

He grins at that, a little dimple popping up on the right side of his cheek, distracting me. "So what about my offer. Do you want to hitch a ride to Vegas?"

His offer sounds tempting, but I really don't know these men, and I'd rather drive there by myself. Even if that means I have to call my dad.

Who am I kidding? While I wouldn't feel comfortable driving to Vegas with Renny and his friends, I'd probably still choose that option over asking Dad for help.

My phone rings, bringing me back to reality, especially when my sister's name pops up on the screen.

Shit.

"Ariel, hello?" I say, raising a finger to Renny apologetically. I turn my back a little for privacy, glancing down at my shoes, silently praying that everything is okay.

"Izzy, have you left? I'm in labor, it wasn't just Braxton Hicks. You need to be here now!" she says in a panic. "The way these contractions are coming on…" She starts to scream in pain, and I hold the phone away from my ear, wincing. "Fuck!"

Man, I am never having a baby if that is what I have to go through. My older sister is one of the strongest women I know, and she has a high pain threshold, so anything that makes her sound like that gets a nope from me.

"I'm leaving now," I promise, turning back to Renny. "I'll be there as soon as I can, Ariel. I love you."

"I love you, too," she says before hanging up.

I weigh my options and the likelihood that I will make it to Vegas in time. I may not know Renny, but I promised Ariel I would be there for the birth of her child. My niece or nephew. And I will not let her down.

"So when are you leaving?" I ask before I can give any more thought to what I am doing. I need to go, and I need to go now. It's a five-hour drive, and maybe, just maybe, I will make it before the baby's head crowns and ruins Ariel's vagina.

"Was going to be in an hour or so, but we can make it right now," he says, pulling out his phone. "I'll tell the men."

"Just how many men are we traveling with?" I ask as he types out a text message. "And what about my suitcase?"

"Three of us, and don't worry, you can trust me, and the rest of them. You'll be safe, I promise you. Skylar can vouch for us, if that makes you feel better," he says, brown eyes pinned on me.

Oddly enough, I believe him. I'm not afraid for my safety around them. I mean they've been my neighbors for over a year and they haven't bothered me once. "Suitcase?"

"We'll get there faster on the bike," he replies with a shrug.

If this means the five-hour drive could be cut shorter, that means I'll get to Ariel sooner. I don't need anything in my suitcase.

"Fuck it," I tell him. "I'll buy new clothes there."

His lip twitches, and he nods toward his black motorcycle. "Get on. I'll try my best to get you there on time."

"Thank you, Renny," I say, grabbing my handbag from my car and crossing the strap over my body. I have my purse, ID and credit cards; anything else can be bought.

"Have you ever ridden before?" he asks as he helps me climb on, his large hands on my waist sending shivers up my spine.

"Yeah, I have actually," I tell him, smiling fondly, remembering the times I'd ride with my cousin before he passed away. "On the back of one, anyway."

"Okay," he murmurs, studying me with a slightly narrowed gaze. I've always had a weakness for men with blue eyes, but suddenly brown is looking extremely appealing. "I'll skip the debrief then. We need to stop at the clubhouse first, but then we will head off. You have the address of where you need to be?"

"Yeah, I do," I reply, reciting the name and address of the hospital to him.

He nods and hands me his spare helmet. "I'll have your car towed to the clubhouse and it should be ready by the time we get back from Vegas."

"That's great. Thank you," I say, feeling grateful it's one less thing to worry about. "I just need to get there."

The thought of Ariel in labor alone makes me feel sick to my stomach. The baby decided to come two weeks early, otherwise I would have been with her this entire time. The father is my sister's ex and wants nothing to do with the baby, which makes my role even more important.

Renny gets on in front of me and fires up the engine. "Let's do it then."

Feeling awkward, I put the helmet on and hold on to the back of his leather vest, very aware of my personal space, knowing that I'm about to be pressed up against this man for the next few hours at least. I'm not exactly sure how I've found myself in this situation, or how this Renny ended up being my knight in shining armor, but I'm glad he was around.

I've heard a lot of things about the MC—like that they engage in criminal activities and are dangerous womanizers. I know they are judged in the community and that no one wants them here, but I want to form my own opinion. Even the real estate agent who sold me my house told me that he wished they would move away, because they are nothing but trouble.

But from what Renny is doing for me, they don't seem too bad.

Or at least I hope they aren't.

Because I just signed up for the next few hours at their mercy.

Ariel, I'm coming.

Chapter Two

We stop at the clubhouse, where I meet Temper, Saint and Dee, our travel companions. While Temper is older and stoic, Dee is kind of goofy and playful, which lightens the mood.

"Trust you to pick up a hot chick to take on the ride," he says to Renny, grinning. "Nice to officially meet you, sweetheart. Please note that I am also single, after my last online dating experience left me feeling lonely and rejected."

Saint, on the other hand, is the epitome of cool. "Do you really say stuff like that to women? No wonder you're single."

"Renny's single," Dee points out.

"By choice," Saint replies with a smirk, bringing his blue eyes to me. "Renny is just waiting for the right woman to come along."

The clubhouse looks completely different than what I had imagined it—it's neat and tidy, for one, decorated very masculinely, but it has a homey feel to it that I didn't expect. Saint thanks me again for helping Skylar, who I learn is his girlfriend, or "old lady" in motorcycle speak, but we don't linger to chat for long because Renny kindly tells them that we're in a rush and need to leave right now, which I appreciate.

"You all ready?" I hear Temper ask the men.

"Yeah, Prez. We're ready," Dee says.

I take in their all-black getup, mostly comprised of leather, and then my light blue skinny jeans and mustard-yellow sweater. Along with my white Converses, I'm going to stand out like a sore thumb on this ride.

"Let me know if you need a break," Renny says as he packs the leather satchel hanging off his bike with water, clothing and his wallet and phone. "We're all used to riding long distances, so we probably won't stop unless you want to."

"Just hit him across the head if you want to stop. He'll get the point," Saint teases with a smirk.

"We definitely have to stop for some food," Dee says, frowning. "What do you mean we ain't stopping?"

I hide my smile at the banter between them. I was expecting a grumpy bunch of brooding assholes, but now I can relax a little. Don't get me wrong, Temper is brooding and kind of scary, but I don't feel like I'm unwanted here, and the men seem to genuinely not mind that I'm tagging along on their road trip. Besides, they seem to speak so highly of Skylar. It's obvious they love and care about her deeply.

Lucky woman.

And I don't think I've ever been so easily accepted in my life.

Bikers, who knew?

"I'm not opposed to a quick food stop," I reply, winking at Dee, who chuckles. These men are all helping me get to where I need to be, and in record time, so a little stop won't kill us. "I'm partial to doughnuts and bagels with extra cream cheese, but I'm not going to say no to any food at any point."

With all the men packed and ready to go in record time, I climb on Renny's bike and hold on to his leather once more.

"You can hold me tighter," he says to me, bringing my arms around his waist. "I'm not going to bite, and you better get comfortable because it's going to be a long ride."

Sliding forward and holding on to him the way he suggested, I try to pretend that I don't notice how hard his stomach is, and nod, even though he can't see me. The familiar rumbles have my own stomach in a knot, because everything just got real.

I'm going on a road trip with the Knights of Fury MC.

I last an hour before my ass starts getting numb and my lower back starts to ache a little, but I don't complain. If I ask Renny to stop more than once or twice, I know it's going to take much longer to get there.

During the ride I worry about Ariel and whether or not the baby has arrived. I'm going to be so sad if I've missed the birth, but it's completely my fault.

I know that some labors can be quick and others can take hours upon hours, so maybe I will make it. Even if I don't, I'll still get to be there with her, see the baby and take care of them both, helping in any way I can. I'm lucky that working as a freelance graphic designer allows me to be flexible with my work and be my own boss.

Not that I brought my laptop, which is packed in my luggage. So apparently I don't plan on working until I get back.

After we've been riding for what seems like ten hours, but is probably only two, Renny stops in front of a gas station and restaurant. I'm off the bike the second it comes to a halt, removing my helmet and shifting on my feet, trying to get the feeling back into the lower half of my body.

Renny takes off his own helmet and studies me. "Why didn't you tell me that you needed to stop? You're stubborn, you know that?"

I do know that, and I don't want to bring up the fact that my lower back isn't my friend right now, so I simply shrug and play it off. "I'm fine."

He purses his lips, clearly disagreeing with me, but he lets it go. "Come on, let's get something to eat."

He holds the door open for me, waiting for me to pass him before also stepping inside.

"Thank you," I say, glancing up at him. Brown eyes watch me a little too closely, but he stays quiet. "I said, thank you," I repeat, arching a brow.

"You're welcome," he replies, lip twitching.

With him standing behind me, I turn and stare up at the menu. I'm starving, but more than anything I need something to drink.

"What do you want?" he asks, coming to stand beside me.

"I can get it," I tell him, frowning. "In fact, I should be buying your lunch since you're the one doing me a favor."

His eyes narrow, and a scowl twists his full lips. "What do you want to eat, Isabella? And don't forget we're on a time crunch, so don't even bother trying to argue because we'll be here all day. I've never let a woman pay for anything for me, and I'm not going to start now."

"What about your mom?" I ask, lifting my chin.

He scrubs his hand down his face and gently pushes me to the front counter with a hand on my lower back. "Tell the lady what you want."

The rest of the men walk in and we all order together. I quickly head to the restroom while we're waiting and send Ariel a text message saying I'm on my way. When I return, they are all sitting at one of the tables with burgers and sodas in front of them.

"How was the ride for you?" Dee asks me, grinning. "I saw you holding on for dear life there."

"It felt like we were going so fast," I tell him, sitting down next to Renny. "But you were going the speed limit."

"Check that, did you?" Renny asks, arching a dark brow.

"Yeah, of course I did. I'm a law-abiding citizen."

They all laugh. Narrowing my green eyes, I look around the table and stare at them each in turn. "What's so funny? I'm being serious."

"Nothing," Renny replies, lips still slightly lifted. "How have we not spoken until today? You're hilarious."

"I guess we run in different circles," I state with a straight face.

More laughter.

"What do you do for work?" Temper asks me, leaning back in his chair.

"I'm a freelance graphic designer," I tell him. "So I'm my own boss, which is pretty cool. What do you all do?"

"We are business owners and entrepreneurs," Dee replies, grinning. "And motorcycle enthusiasts, of course."

"Of course," I say, laughing softly. "Any businesses I would have heard of?"

"You want us to give away all of our secrets right off the bat?" Renny teases, lifting his coffee cup to his lips and taking a sip. He's a smooth operator, this Renny, and I knew that from the second he first spoke to me. He has a lot of swag to him—every move is sensual, graceful and…just cool.

"Sure. You can tell me all of your real names while you're at it," I throw in, flashing them a sweet smile.

They laugh, so I'm guessing that's a no.

Renny is a cool guy, and I find myself wanting to press my palm against his stubble to see what it feels like. I'm a very affectionate, touchy-feely type of person, but now is not the time, especially in front of all these men, and this is not the man for me to push boundaries with. He's a friend, helping me out because I helped one of their women, and nothing more. He's the last type of man I need to be showing any interest in.

"I guess I can wait until the ride home," I say nonchalantly.

We eat our food quickly before getting back on the road. This time when I hold on to Renny, I don't feel as shy or as awkward, in fact, I enjoy being pressed up against him, and even though my mind is with my sister, I allow myself to enjoy the moment.

After all, it's not every day that you have a good-looking biker escorting you to another state.

Chapter Three

By the time we pull up to the hospital, I'm utterly exhausted, and all I had to do was sit and hold on for the entire ride. I can only imagine how Renny feels. Still, excitement fills me, and I can't wait to run inside and see Ariel. Jumping off the bike, I remove my helmet and hand it to Renny.

"Thank you so much for getting me here," I say, stepping closer and giving him a warm hug. "You're a lifesaver."

"You're welcome. Why don't you give me your number and message me whenever you need a lift home? We'll be here," he says, pulling out his phone.

"Are you sure?" I ask, feeling bad that he's going to try to work around my schedule for when I want to leave.

"Yeah, I'm sure," he assures me, running his hand through his dark, messy hair. "We got you here, and we'll get you home, too."

I tell him my number and he saves it into his phone. Waving goodbye to him and the other guys, I run into the hospital and ask for my sister at the front desk.

"Room fifteen," the nurse tells me and points down the hall to the right.

"Thank you," I call out as I start to jog to the room.

Looking up at the number fifteen, I knock on the door quietly. I don't hear her screaming; the room silent. When the door opens, I see Ariel looking tired but beautiful, and a gorgeous baby wrapped up in a pink blanket.

I missed it. For a small moment, I'm sad that I couldn't be there for Ariel and welcome my niece into the world. But I'm here now, and I'm going to make up for it.

"Sorry I'm late," I say to Ariel, bending down to give her a kiss on her forehead. "You look too beautiful to have just given birth."

She smiles, and glances down at her daughter. *Daughter*, that sounds so crazy. "Isn't she amazing, Izzy?"

"She's perfect," I reply, holding my arms out so I can carry her. Ariel hands her over to me and I sit down with her in my arms, tears threatening to fall from my eyes as I stare down at my niece.

"You are so loved," I whisper to her, gently trailing my finger down her soft, chubby cheek. I now know that love at first sight is a very real thing, because there's nothing I wouldn't do for this little girl in my arms.

Nothing.

"And so beautiful. What did you name her?" I ask, gently rocking as she starts to fuss. "Did you go with any of the names we had on the list?"

We've been compiling this list since we were little, the names on it always changing whenever we hear a new one we love.

"I did. Mila Isabella," she says, beaming.

"You gave her my name?" I whisper, blinking quickly as this time the tears do fall, dripping down my cheeks. "If it's possible, I love her more now."

Ariel laughs, and then tells me about her labor, which lasted about three hours. "I sent you a message to tell you that she had arrived, but you must not have checked your phone. But you got here pretty fast."

"I rode here on a motorcycle," I drop casually, handing her back Mila when she starts to cry, probably hungry.

Ariel takes her daughter to feed her. "What do you mean you rode here on a motorcycle?"

"Well, when I was about to leave my car decided to break down," I start, leaning back in the chair and studying her. "I had two options. One, to try to get it fixed quickly then drive, or two, try to book a flight, but you know how I feel about planes."

Although I did have a third option, and probably the easiest one, which was to call my father and ask him for his help.

But my pride wouldn't let me even consider that option.

It's actually pretty sad, because he should be here, present for his firstborn daughter giving birth to his first grandchild, but he's not.

"You would have gotten on a plane for me?" she asks, green eyes going wide, knowing my terrible fear of flying. "If that's not love, I don't know what is."

"If I had no other option, then yes, I would have." But I wouldn't have liked it.

"But you didn't come in your car…"

"Nope. One of the bikers next door saw me on the side of the road, offered to help fix my car and give me a ride to you. They were already heading in this direction, so made a slight detour for me," I explain, laughing at the look of shock on her face.

"You let one of the bikers from the MC near your house drive you all the way here? And he did it from the kindness of his heart?" she reaffirms, brow furrowing. "And he just happened to be riding toward Vegas?"

"Yes, yes and yes," I reply, shrugging. "You have serious trust issues, you know that? I helped one of their girlfriends out. Do you know they actually call their girlfriends 'old ladies'? Can you believe that?" Ariel is still looking at me like I grew a second head. "I needed to be here, Ariel. I hated the thought of you having to be in labor alone, and after everything, you had to do it alone anyway. I'm sorry."

She waves her hand in the air, dismissing my concerns. "I was fine, Izzy. I was in so much pain I couldn't really think of much else, and you're here now, which is all that matters to me. I know how much you wanted to be here. I mean, shit, you even took a ride with some random criminal biker to get here."

Shaking my head with a grin playing on my lips, I add, "Yeah, and I didn't bring my suitcase so I have nothing except my handbag and the clothes on my back, so I'm going to need to borrow some shit."

She laughs softly. "You can go to my place and borrow whatever you need. My car is in the hospital parking lot."

"You drove yourself here?" I ask, feeling like absolute shit.

"Yeah," she says, scanning my eyes. "Izzy, it was fine. I only live ten minutes from here and the contractions weren't too bad when I drove in."

"I feel so bad."

"You can't help that Mila decided to come early," she says, looking down at the baby with awe in her face.

"I know," I mutter, but I still hate the fact she went through this time alone. "You never should have moved out here."

Ariel moved to Vegas to be with Merve, her then boy-friend and Mila's father, but they broke up when he found out she was pregnant, and she hasn't heard from him since.

"I know. Actually I think I'm going to move back home to California in a few months, when Mila is a little older," she says to me. "I'll need some time to pack my house up and sell everything."

"I'll help you with whatever you need," I promise. "And there's a spare room at my house with your and Mila's names all over it."

"You sure?" she asks, brows drawing together. "You going to be able to live with a crying baby? You work from home. It will probably drive you crazy."

"I'm sure," I reply, scowling at her for second-guessing it. "I'd love the company, and even if she cries all night, we can take shifts so we both get some sleep. We'll work it out. I'd love having you both there, Ariel. I can't think of anything better."

She smiles, eyes lighting up.

She might be my older sister, but I've always looked after her, and I always will.

"Did you call Dad?" I ask, not sure if she was going to want him to come and visit her or not.

"I sent him a message, but he didn't reply," she admits, shrugging. "Either he's busy or he just doesn't care."

Our dad has been so in and out of our lives that it's hard to keep up. You'd think for this occasion he'd put in the effort, though, and be on a plane, but you never know with him. How much interest he shows in us usually depends on his own agenda, and it's always been that way. We've always come second to his career, but when he left our mom for his now wife, we became lower on his list of importance. Even more so now that he has kids with her.

I remember once sending him a copy of my report card when I was twelve, hoping he would be proud and want to see us more, but the next time I saw him he asked me why I didn't get an A in math. I had gotten a B, and even though the rest of my report card was straight As, that's the grade he had to point out.

That's the kind of man he is.

"It's his loss. Can I hold her again?" I ask after Mila finishes eating.

"Sure," Ariel replies with a yawn. "Maybe I'll have a nap now, knowing she is in safe hands."

I lift her up from my sister and cradle her against my chest. "She's so little," I whisper, sitting back down and smiling at her. "I can't believe you made this. I think she looks just like you, too. Maybe even better looking."

"And look at you being so complimentary with her," Ariel laughs, while I roll my eyes. It's a known fact that I struggle giving compliments to people, but that clearly doesn't apply with babies. It's a weird thing to have an issue with but with my family history, can you blame me?

I can't believe Merve is missing all of this. If I ever see that man… Let's just say I'm going to show him my old Muay Thai moves.

It doesn't matter, though, because Mila is going to be the most loved child who ever did exist, and she doesn't need Merve, because she's not going to miss out on a single thing.

"She even has the same birthmark as you, the one inside her wrist," I point out, glancing up at Ariel to find her already fast asleep.

The poor thing must be exhausted. She should be so

proud of herself and everything she has accomplished all on her own, without ever complaining once. She worked throughout her pregnancy as a legal secretary, saving money for when Mila came along, and I never ever heard her even say she was tired.

She is Superwoman.

"I guess it's just me and you now, little one," I say, running my thumb along Mila's birthmark.

I've never felt more content.

Chapter Four

Unlocking the door, I step into Ariel's apartment and take a look around. The place is just as I remembered it, a two-bedroom, one-bathroom apartment that is quite luxurious and spacious. My sister has a completely different taste in interior design to me, hers more natural, with neutral colors and modern elegance.

Yawning, tired after the ride and spending a few hours with Ariel and Mila, I head toward her room, searching through her dresser. Finding some jeans and a top, I head into the bathroom and turn on the shower. I've been looking forward to this moment. Putting some music on my phone, I undress and step under the scalding water, closing my eyes and tipping my head backward.

What a day. So much has happened in such a short period of time, and it's nice to have a silent moment to just process the whole thing.

I'm an aunty. It's still so hard to wrap my head around it.

Once I'm dry and dressed, silently thankful that Ariel and I are the same size, I tidy up her kitchen, which she must have left in a rush, the dishes in the sink and toast on a plate. The rest of the apartment is spotless, and I'd expect nothing else from Ariel, her obsessive neatness well-known. When my phone vibrates with a text message from an unknown number, butterflies find their way into my stomach.

You all good?

I'm assuming it's from Renny, checking in, or at least I'm hoping so, but I message back asking just to make sure. Renny?

How many other guys from random numbers do you have texting you?

I laugh and type out, Too many to count.

I told the men you weren't as sweet as you seem.

Unable to stop the smile on my face, I jump up on the counter and type back. Apparently you're smarter than you look.

I don't know if I've crossed the line with that one, roasting a scary biker guy, but he just comes off as fun and playful and I don't feel scared of him at all.

Smartass.

Phew.

Yes, I'm all good, and a very proud aunty.

Congrats. Let me know if you ever need anything. We're staying in Vegas for a little while.

I'm good, but thank you. I think I might stay here another week to spend time with my sister and help her out.

Sounds good. Message me the day you want to leave and the address and we will be there.

He's like my very own Uber.

I reply with a thank-you, jump down off the counter and grab the few things Ariel asked me to bring back to the hospital—an extra pair of pajamas, her phone charger, some books and some snacks that I'm meant to smuggle in—and then head back to her.

Ariel and Mila are both fast asleep when I get there, so I curl up on the chair with a book and watch over them.

And I don't mind for a second that this is going to be my life over the next week.

After two nights in the hospital, Ariel is given the all clear to go home with Mila. With the nursery all set up and waiting, I decide to cook in bulk and do some food prep to freeze for her so she will have prepared meals when I leave.

"You don't have to do that, Izzy," Ariel says as she watches me with Mila in her arms. "I want you to relax. I didn't ask you to come here to be my house elf."

"I want to," I tell her, continuing to chop vegetables without missing a beat. "Let me look after you. It's the least I can do considering I won't be here to help you until you move back home." I pause, and then add, "Actually I could come back here. I just need to go home and get my laptop so I can do some work."

"Who's the older sister here?"

"Don't worry, if I ever have a baby, I'm going to expect you to return the favor. Tenfold," I tease, placing the knife down and washing my hands in the sink. "Do we have everything you need for Mila? Or do we need to go on a shopping trip? I still want to buy her a gift."

"You sent her a box of stuff," she argues, shaking her head. "You literally bought her most of the clothes she has to wear for the next six months. What else does she need?"

"Clothes to wear after six months?"

"You're terrible, you know that? You should be saving your money," she chastises, gently tapping Mila on the back to burp her. "Mila has everything that she needs."

"I finally have a niece, Ariel. Do you know how long I've been waiting for this moment? Don't try to steal it from me," I fire back, sticking my tongue out at her. "I only wish Mom was here to see her. She would have simply adored her."

Ariel goes silent, and I instantly regret saying anything.

We lost our mom to cancer four years ago, and it was the hardest thing we've ever been through in our lives. I still miss her every day, but especially in moments like these. She raised us all by herself for the most part, and we were all really close, always just us three, having each other's back through everything life would throw at us.

The cancer was the one thing that won.

"I know," Ariel finally whispers. "And Mila will know it, too."

I lean forward and kiss the top of Mila's dark, fuzzy head. "Yes, she will. Now, why don't you go and rest? Or have a nap? I read that you're meant to sleep while she does. I'm going to be in the kitchen for the next few hours getting all of this sorted."

"Are you chasing me from my own kitchen?" she jokes, yawning. "I love you, you know that?"

"I do know that," I reply, grinning.

She flashes me a sleepy smile, and then heads to her room with Mila, leaving me to cook up a storm. She's still asleep when I'm done, so I plop down on the couch and check my phone, laughing when I see a picture that Renny sent me, one of him with one of those giant alcoholic slushy drinks, the caption reading When in Vegas.

It's not a selfie, so one of the other guys must have taken it. I can't imagine Renny taking a selfie, he doesn't seem like the type. But me, on the other hand, I have no problem doing so, so I send one back of me in my pajamas with the caption Not the usual Vegas experience. I didn't expect him to maintain any contact, and especially not to send any pictures, giving me insight into what he's doing, but I kind of like that he is.

"What are you getting yourself into, Izzy?" I mutter to myself. I know it sounds like a bad idea having any involvement with a motorcycle club, not that I know anything about them other than what I see in the media, or the whispers I've heard from the locals. But once you meet and hang out with these guys it's so different, and doesn't feel like you're at all doing anything wrong. At the end of the day, they are my closest neighbors and I should be on good terms with them, friends even, but that's probably where the boundary line should stay. That would be the smart thing to do.

Friends message each other, though, right?

And send cute pics to each other.

Mila starts to cry a little later, so I rush into her nursery and pick her up, hoping Ariel stays asleep so she can get some more rest.

"Hello, beautiful," I whisper, cradling her and breathing in her baby scent. She stops crying as soon as I pick her up, so I sit back down on the couch and have a cuddle. Just as I sit there's a knock at the door, so I quickly move toward it, frowning when I glance through the peephole and see Merve standing there, the bastard.

"What do you want?" I call out, scowling. There's no way in hell I'm letting him in here, especially without the okay from Ariel. From what I've seen and heard of this man, he's unpredictable, and I'm not going to put my sister and niece at risk.

"I heard that Ariel had the baby and I want to see it," he replies, stepping back and crossing his arms over his chest. "Let me in, Izzy. They are my family."

Family? This man wouldn't know what that was if it hit him in the face, which it just might. I can't believe the nerve of him. This is the man who deserted Ariel when she found out she was pregnant. The man who hasn't shown any interest in being a father, never mind giving zero support to my sister in any emotional or financial way. If you look up *Deadbeat Dad*, a mug shot of this guy will show up.

I cover Mila's ears and tell him to kindly fuck off.

The commotion wakes up Ariel, who walks out of her room looking like she had a good sleep, her dark hair sticking up in every direction. "Who are you telling to fuck off?" she whisper-yells.

Merve, I mouth to her, glancing down at Mila. "What the fuck is he doing here?"

She looks as confused as me. "He must have heard I had the baby."

"From who? You have no friends here," I whisper back at her, frowning.

"I made a social media post." She shrugs, regret flashing in her eyes. "I didn't think he'd show up. Why would he? He's been missing in action for eight months now, but someone must have told him."

"What should we do?" I ask, pursing my lips. "I vote for calling the cops."

"I can hear you guys," Merve calls out through the door. "Can you let me in, please? I just want to see her. I am her father, after all."

Ariel and I share a look.

"I told you that you should have gotten a German shepherd, or something," I mutter, gritting my teeth. "Then we could have just let it loose on him."

"I can still hear you," he continues.

"I don't give a fuck," I call back, still covering Mila's ears, like she'd understand the obscenities leaving my lips. "What do you want to do?" I ask Ariel. As much as I want to tell him to take a hike, I know it's not my decision here.

"Should we just let him in? He can see her and then leave. I have no doubt he won't want to step up and be a father, so it might get rid of him," she suggests, coming forward and taking Mila.

"It's your call," I tell her, but really I want her to just tell him to fuck off. It's going to be like this for the rest of Mila's life, him coming in and out whenever he feels like it, I just know it. He is her father, though, so I know that that means something to Ariel, especially growing up without a father for most of our lives. She wouldn't want Mila to grow up without a father, but who needs a man who doesn't give his whole heart over to his child?

"Shit," she whispers, then steps toward the door. "If you try any bullshit, I'm going to call the cops, Merve!"

"No bullshit, I just want to see her," he says back. I'll admit, he sounds sincere enough, but the man is a master manipulator.

Ariel opens the door and he steps inside, eyes on his daughter. I take a step closer to her, my protective instincts kicking in.

"Can I hold her?" he asks, holding out his arms. Merve is a good-looking man. A little too good-looking, which should have been the first hint that he was going to turn out to be a douche, but at least Mila got some pretty genes running through her.

"Sit down," Ariel tells him, glancing down at her daughter, hesitating. She sighs, takes a deep breath and then hands her over to him, making sure that he's supporting her neck and holding her correctly.

"She's adorable," he says, smiling down at Mila. There seems to be some emotion in his gaze, so maybe he does care for her. I guess only time will tell.

"How did you know Ariel had her?" I ask, studying him closely.

"Gina told me," he explains, referring to one of their mutual friends. "She said you named her Mila. Beautiful name."

My jaw goes tight. How dare he step up in here like he has every right, and act like father of the fucking year? Ariel's expression tells me that she's highly unimpressed, too, but I know she's trying to be mature about the situation and handle everything the best way she can. She's going to have to deal with this for the rest of her life, forever tied to him through her daughter.

"Yes, her name is Mila Isabella," she says, tapping her foot on the floor. "And what do you want from us exactly, Merve? Do you want to be in her life? Or are you going to just drop by whenever you feel like acknowledging her? Because we need to do whatever is best for her, not what's best for you."

"I don't know," he admits, which is at least honest, but doesn't sound promising. "I just knew that I had to see her. She's my child, too, Ariel, but I have a lot going on in my life right now and I don't know if I'm cut out for the whole father thing. My business is just taking off, and that needs to be my focus right now. I'll come and see her when I can."

My fingers close into a fist. I know that some might have sympathy for him and his situation, but I have nothing. My sister is the hero in this story, and Merve has done nothing but think about himself, not wanting to give up his playboy lifestyle for changing diapers and supporting a baby.

"What are you doing?" she asks as he pulls out his phone.

"Taking a photo of her to show my family," he says, capturing the image of her in his arms. "They will want to see her, too."

"The same family that hasn't made contact once to ask about her?" I blurt out, unable to hold my tongue. "Or to see if Ariel is healthy, or needs anything?"

"This has nothing to do with you, Izzy," Merve growls, sliding his phone back into his shirt pocket and pinning me with a death stare.

"You sure? Because I'm more her parent than you've been," I fire back, daring him to challenge me again.

He stands and hands Mila back to Ariel. "I'll be back to see her."

He doesn't say when, so I guess it's going to be whenever he feels like it. He's such a piece of shit. We both watch him leave the house, then lock the door behind him.

"I don't regret Mila, but boy, do I regret sleeping with that man," Ariel mutters, sighing deeply and looking worried. "It was easier when I thought he was hiding from us."

"If you hit him up for child support, I'm sure he will," I tease, sitting down. "I'll bet you any money he will post the pictures on social media and have everyone commenting about how cute she is. He's probably acting like a proud, involved father."

"Some people have no shame," she groans, shaking her head and sitting down next to me. "Thanks for having my back. It would have been so much worse if you weren't here."

I reach over and touch her hand. "I'm always in your corner."

Because that is what family is for.

Chapter Five

The rest of the week passes quickly, with no more drama from Merve. In fact, we don't hear from him at all. I don't know if I should be annoyed or relieved, but I think it's the latter.

Ariel settles into motherhood like a pro, and I feel sad that I have to leave her, but I really do need to get back to work and my home.

"Are you sure you don't want to come with me?" I ask, frowning. "You can stay at my house for a while."

She shakes her head. "I'll be fine, Izzy. I need to start packing and tie all loose ends here before I move back. I have enough money saved that I don't need to work for a few months at least, so I'm good. I don't want to rush around right now. I just want to spend this time bonding with Mila and enjoying being a mom without any unnecessary stress."

"Okay, but you say the word and I'm coming to get you," I promise, pausing and then adding, "The second I get my car fixed."

She laughs. "Let me know if you need some money."

"I'll be fine," I tell her, using her words back at her. "I have a lot of work lined up." That I probably should have been doing this whole time.

"That's good, because you're super talented and if I were you I'd be raising my prices."

"You're my sister, you have to say that." I grin, wrapping my arm around her. "I'm going to miss you and Mila so much."

"Me, too, but I will be seeing you soon enough," she promises, looking toward the door when she hears the sound of rumbling motorcycles. "Looks like your ride is here. Are you sure you trust them?"

"They brought me here in one piece, didn't they?" I remind her, picking up my handbag and draping it over my shoulder.

"Yeah, I guess so. I'm just a little concerned that you might be taking 'love thy neighbor' a little too literally," she grumbles, moving toward the front door with me.

"What do you mean?"

"You're crushing on Renny," she says, frowning like it's obvious. "And don't act like you're not. You smile like an idiot every time he messages you, and you talk about him a lot. And I'm your big sister, you can't fool me."

I open my mouth and then close it. "I think he's a nice guy, yes."

"He's a biker," she reminds me.

"The two aren't mutually exclusive," I say, rolling my eyes.

"I know, I'm just a little worried. You're out there on your own, and if something happens, I'm hours away. Just how much do you know about these men because you're putting an awful amount of trust in them? Is it dangerous being tied to them? I don't know what to expect with this whole revelation."

She's right, and I know it. I *am* trusting them, but

they haven't given me any reason not to as of yet, and I'm running with it.

"I feel the same about you, which is why I was suggesting that you move home sooner," I point out, touching her shoulder and sighing. "I'll be fine, the bikers won't do anything to hurt me, and you'll be fine, too. Merve might go MIA again so he doesn't have to pay any child support, and then soon enough we'll be living together and can be so far up each other's business that we wish we lived in separate states again."

"Sounds like the perfect plan," she replies, smiling widely.

I rush to the nursery and kiss a sleeping Mila goodbye, and then head out front, where Ariel has boldly already gone, staring down the men. They all stay on their bikes except for Renny, who approaches us both, helmet in hand.

"Hello," he says to Ariel, offering her his hand. "I'm Renny."

"Ariel," my sister introduces herself, and I don't miss the firm grip she offers him. "You'll get her home safely, won't you?"

"Of course," he replies, nodding. "We would never let anything bad happen to her. You have my word."

She lifts her phone up and takes a photo of him. "Good, but just in case something does happen to her, this is the photo I'm going to show the police so they can hunt your ass down."

Renny tries to contain his amusement, but I don't miss the flash of it in his eyes. "I'll remember that, but you have nothing to worry about. I'm sure she will check in with you so you don't have to worry."

"I will," I promise Ariel, giving her the biggest hug

and kissing her on the cheek. "I love you, and I will call you as soon as I get home, all right?"

"Okay," she says, sounding a little emotional. "Thank you for everything."

"You don't need to thank me," I tell her, stepping back and smiling. "What's family for, right? Love you!"

"Love you, too, baby sis," she says back.

I wave at the other men, then get on the bike and put my helmet on, once again pressed up against Renny.

I keep my eyes on my sister until she's out of my sight, waving goodbye to her, and then look ahead. We'll be reunited soon enough, and I know that, but it still sucks leaving her alone with her daughter when I know she doesn't have anyone around to help. Sure, she has a few friends, but nothing compares to family.

Renny and the guys soon make a pit stop, parking their bikes near a busy street.

"What are we doing?" I ask, taking my helmet off and fixing my hair.

"Thought we'd get something to eat," he says, offering me his hand. "It's going to be a long ride home. You aren't in any rush, are you?"

I shake my head. "I guess not." Food sounds good, and because we were so busy with Mila, Ariel and I didn't exactly get to explore Vegas or do anything adult-y, so it's kind of nice to get out.

"How was your visit?" Temper asks as Renny and I reach him.

"Really good. How was yours?" I ask. I'm not sure what they did or where they went, and I doubt I'm going to get much of an explanation, but I'm not really expecting one. Temper does look to be in a good mood, though, so maybe he got laid or something.

"Uneventful, but relaxing. It's nice to get away," is his reply.

"It is," I agree.

We walk toward the Strip, me in the middle with Renny and Temper on each side of me, Dee and Saint on the outskirts, and I don't miss the looks everyone is giving us.

"Must be the all black and leather," I mutter, glancing down at what must be the signature look of Renny and the other men, and back at my new ripped jeans and denim jacket. Underneath is my sister's royal blue top, one I've been eying for a while that she finally let me steal.

Renny glances over at me and winks. "You sure they're all looking at us?"

"Yes." I nod. "Or maybe they're wondering if you're holding me hostage, or something."

The men laugh, but hey, it could be true. I'm surrounded by dangerous-looking men, and everyone must be able to tell that there's something about them, and not just because of the leather cuts they are wearing. They are just a bunch of strong, tall, dominant alpha males, and anyone can see that from a quick glance.

"What do you feel like eating?" Renny asks, glancing at the many options.

"How about that place?" I suggest, pointing to a pub.

"You always surprise me, you know that?" he murmurs, shaking his head. "I thought you'd choose something like that." He points to some posh, expensive-looking restaurant.

"Someone needs to keep you on your toes," I reply, feeling bold and oddly comfortable. We get a table at the back, and order food and drinks.

"You better not have too many of those," Renny quips,

watching me take a sip of my mango daiquiri. "Pretty sure your sister will skin me alive if you fall off my bike because you're drunk."

"I can't go to Vegas and not have one alcoholic beverage," I state. "It would just be rude, don't you think?"

When Renny and the rest of the men order water, or soda, I feel like I may be the bad influence at the table. When my steak arrives, though, I know that it's going to soak up any ounce of alcohol in my system, because it is *huge*.

"There's no way you're going to eat all that," Renny remarks.

"Your eyes are bigger than your stomach," Dee adds, chuckling. "That steak is the size of your head."

"How was I supposed to know it was going to be this big?" I defend, picking up my knife and fork and studying it.

"I bet she doesn't even get halfway through it," Renny declares, unknowingly tapping into my competitive side. "I'm calling it now."

"I'm going to prove you wrong," I tell him, cutting into it. "You obviously haven't seen a Beck woman eat before. Me, my sister, and even my mom when she was alive—all big eaters."

"Where the hell does the food go?" Dee asks, frowning.

"To all the right places," I think I hear Renny mutter, but I can't be sure.

"What did you say?"

"Nothing," he says quickly, drinking from his water. "You much of a gambler?"

"I've never gambled before," I admit to him. "I don't have much luck."

"You've never gambled before?" he repeats, looking

shell-shocked. "But you have family in Vegas. How many times have you been here?"

"A couple," I admit, shrugging. "My sister isn't really the partying type, so I've never even checked out any of the clubs here."

They all stare at me, dumbfounded.

"You know what, fuck it," Renny says, glancing around the table. "We need to show her how to do Vegas, the right way. A little gambling, a few drinks, and a hell of a lot of food."

I hate to admit that I'm tempted, and I wouldn't say no to spending more time with Renny before I'm back to reality. "What do you have in mind?"

He calls over the waitress and orders the table a round of beers, then turns back to me. "You okay with us going home tomorrow morning instead?"

I don't know what comes over me. I know that I should tell them no, that this isn't the best idea, but I don't want to. I want some excitement, and I want to experience a fun night out in Vegas which, according to them, I'm really missing out on. When I lost my mom, my party days came to an end, and I guess I've just kind of become a boring adult who spends all her time working, and whose idea of a fun time is eating out and online shopping.

Fuck it.

I deserve to let loose.

"Yeah, I'm okay with that," I reply, anticipation filling me.

"Fuck, here we go," Temper grumbles, but accepts the beer that's handed to him and takes a quick drink. "You sure you want to do this, Isabella?"

"I'm intrigued now," I tell him, taking a big bite of

steak. "You only live once, right? And call me Izzy, everyone does."

I think that's the first time I've ever used the saying YOLO, but it's never been so fitting. It's been a long time since I've let loose, had a few drinks and danced the right away, and I think it's just what the doctor ordered.

Right after I demolish this steak.

Chapter Six

"What are these?" Renny asks, taking the shots I hand him.

I deadpan, "Wet pussies."

He almost chokes, making me laugh hard, alcohol dripping down my hands. "Taste them, they are amazing."

He downs the two shots and lands them on the bar. "Not bad."

After finishing my steak and impressing the table, we had a few drinks then headed to the casino, where Renny tried to teach me the ways of gambling, starting with roulette. I'm not going to lie, it's definitely not my thing, but he did prove me wrong about not having any luck. Somehow I turned fifty dollars into seven hundred. Still, he hasn't let me pay for anything all night, and told me not to waste my winnings.

"Your lips say not bad, but your sour expression says that a wet pussy isn't your cup of tea," I reply, laughing harder when I realize how that sounded.

"I don't think any women who know me would say that." He smirks, amusement dancing in his brown eyes. He leans his elbow on the bar, facing me. "Are you having a good night?"

"Are you kidding me? I won money and have eaten and drunk my way down the Strip. Not to mention that somehow you guys have all the right connections and we don't have to even line up anywhere or pay for entry. This is like the VIP treatment."

"With the way that you look, Izzy, trust me, I doubt you'd be lining up or paying for anything here," he says, scanning the dance floor.

"The way I look? I'm dressed in casual clothes, Renny. I was expecting a ride home, not a night on the town, and now I look extremely out of place."

The women around me are dolled up to the nines, with short dresses, stiletto heels and makeup and hair that looks professionally done, and I'm here in jeans, a blue top and rosy cheeks from alcohol instead of product.

"Yet you're still the most beautiful woman in the room," he states, offering me his hand. I know I'm not an unattractive woman, but if he honestly thinks that, he must be blind. There are more beautiful women here tonight than I've ever seen in one place at the same time, but I guess that's Vegas for you.

"I love this song. Do you want to dance?"

"Depends. Are you a good dancer?" I ask, teasing him, but taking his hand at the same time. He pulls me to the busy dance floor and presses against me, not too close, which I like, just enough that it's sexy, and I can feel how his body moves.

"I've heard I'm pretty good," he whispers into my ear, sending shivers down my spine. "But why don't you tell me?"

I can tell instantly that he's right, he does know his way around a dance floor. He moves sensually, in rhythm to the music, but doesn't overdo it, so it doesn't even look like he's trying. It just comes natural to him.

Lifting my arms above my head, I spin around and

press my ass against him, gyrating my hips. I haven't danced with a man like this in years, and it feels so freeing, so…naughty. Which is kind of sad, because lots of people do stuff like this every weekend. I'm buzzing from the alcohol and suddenly life has never been easier, or more fun.

I can see why people like to party.

Renny spins me back around and cups my cheek, smiling at me. "Looks like I've finally met my match."

"Impressed, are you?" I ask, placing my palms on his chest and slowing down my moves. "I used to be a dancer in high school."

"I believe it," he says, and my eyes lower to his lips. Perfect, full, kissable lips. I bet he'd be an amazing kisser, too. I bet he'd be amazing at everything.

"We should have another drink," I tell him, because that suddenly sounds like a wonderful idea. "My treat."

"Nice try," he says, following behind me back to the bar.

I order us another round, this time vodka mixed with an energy drink—because that's always a good idea—and two shots on the side. Renny, clearly more responsible than me, also adds two bottles of water onto the order.

"So is Renny your real name? I mean, I've heard of the name Remy, but not Renny, or is that just short for something?" I ask, tilting my head to the side and studying him. At this point I have no filter, and am probably making no sense, but I want to know everything about this enigma of a man while I have the chance. While there are no guards up between us. Who knows if I will ever get another chance like this?

"No, it's not my birth name, actually," he admits, lifting his drink to his mouth and taking a sip. When he licks a drop off his lips, my thighs squeeze together of their own accord.

Control yourself, Izzy.

"What is it then?" I push.

"Jasper," he answers, lips kicking up at the corners. "Jasper Steel."

My eyes widen. "Why do they call you Renny?"

"It's short for Renegade," he admits, ducking his head as he says it.

"So they gave you a nickname of a nickname?" I ask, smiling with him. "Well, Jasper, I happen to think that's a great name for you."

"No one has called me that in years," he states, running his hand over the stubble on his cheek. "Almost seems like a different person."

"So why Renegade?" I ask, downing my shot and placing it back down on the bar. "Or do these biker road names get chosen at random?"

He laughs at that. "Something like that. Do you want to go and sit back at the table?"

I nod and let him lead me back to where the other guys are all sitting, drinking a bottle of expensive whiskey. Temper has a woman trying to get his attention, but he's flat out ignoring her, concentrating on his phone instead.

"Having a good night?" I ask him over the music.

He puts his phone down and replaces it with his glass. "Trying to. This is not really my scene."

"Really? I couldn't tell," I reply sarcastically, studying him. He's a good-looking man, but it's like he either doesn't notice that or he doesn't care. Either way, there's something about him that screams power, and it's almost like the women around him can sense that straight away. "There's so many women staring at you."

His brows come together, like he's confused. "You're drunk."

"I am, but it's still the truth," I tell him, leaning back onto Renny. "They stare at all of you. It's weird."

"Maybe they're staring at you," Dee states, shrugging and flashing me a charming smile. "Wondering what you have that they don't."

"A broken-down car and luck," I reply, making him laugh. "And damn, Dee, you have a healthy ego on you, don't you?"

He laughs again at that.

"You have much more than that," Renny says, pushing my hair back behind my ear. "Don't forget, you're also our neighbor."

I nudge him with my elbow and roll my eyes at his smartass comment. "I just want to say thank you for taking me out and allowing me to let loose. I'm almost embarrassed to admit how long it's been since the last time I went out and had some fun, so thank you for bringing me here and showing me a good time. And thank you for taking me back tomorrow, when I'm going to be hungover and a huge pain in the ass."

"And thank you for being a fuckin' awesome neighbor and never complaining about the loud bikes and music," Renny replies, casually wrapping his arm around me. "And for giving us some eye candy every time we need to drive down the road and you're out the front of your house."

"Man, he almost crashed that time you were out washing your car," Dee adds, laughing at Renny. "I was right behind him, and the bastard swerved and almost went into a tree."

I chance a look at Renny's expression, which is extremely unimpressed with his friend. "Is that true?"

He shakes his head but grins, giving himself away. "You were in a fuckin' red bikini. How could I not almost crash my bike?"

Resting my cheek against his shoulder, I can't contain my smile. "That's a pretty cute compliment."

He brings his eyes to mine. "You're a pretty cute woman."

"And it wasn't a red bikini, it was a one-piece," I point out, smirking. "And I'd just gotten home from the beach, so the car was filthy."

"Hey, you don't need to make any excuses," Renny adds, bringing his glass to his lips.

I look down and realize that I've finished the drink I had in my hand. "More shots?"

Renny shakes his head at me, so Dee steps up and offers to take me to the bar. "Let her live a little, brother," he says, nodding toward me. "It's her first night out in fuck knows how long, and we're all here to look after her, so nothing can happen to her. Let her be wild for one night, before she's back to being responsible."

"Come on, Renny, have some fun," I say, offering my hand and pulling him up from the booth to come and join us at the bar. "Let's have one more drink and one more dance, and then we can go if you like."

Famous last words.

Chapter Seven

I wake up with the hangover of all hangovers, my head feeling like it's splitting in half. Why do I make such bad decisions? It's like one taste of freedom and I just run with it, going way overboard and having just a little bit too much fun. This is what happens when you don't go out in a long time, or at least where I'm concerned, apparently.

Lifting my head and forcing my eyes open, I glance around the empty hotel room.

A *really* nice, empty hotel room.

Man, it's lovely having rich friends.

Everything hurts as I sit up, my whole body hating me for drinking so much last night and being so irresponsible. When I see Renny asleep on the floor next to the bed, I glance down to make sure that I'm dressed, which I am, but not in last night's clothes. I'm wearing what must be one of Renny's T-shirts. It's black and loose on me. I'm wearing panties and no bra.

Drunk me got really comfortable last night.

Feeling parched, I reach over for a bottle of water next to my bed, crack it open and drink half. My loud swallowing rouses Renny, who sits up and glances around the room, eyes narrowed as they land on me.

I hand him the other half of the water, which he drinks greedily. "Remind me never to party with you again. I feel like crap."

"How was this my fault?" I grumble, sliding back into bed and under the sheets. "This was not my idea."

"The shots were." He groans, standing up in nothing but a pair of black boxer shorts to walk to the bathroom. My eyes widen as I take in his body in all its bare glory— the tattoos, the muscles, the toned, smooth skin. When he turns around, I see the huge knight on his back, the same one I've seen on the leather cut he wears.

He's a beast, a machine, a piece of fucking artwork.

I don't realize my mouth is open until he glances over and catches me looking at him. He points a finger at me, brown eyes narrowed to slits. "Don't you look at me like that."

I close my mouth, and then open it again. "I need a shower, food and some painkillers."

And I mean, I wouldn't say no to a little foreplay with Renny, with him looking like that. I mean, I'm sure it would make me feel better to have his body pressed up against mine, my fingers exploring that Knight while his explore my…

Bang. Bang. Bang.

The loud knock has me jumping and pulling the covers up to cover everything but my head.

Renny answers the door but only opens it a little, so no one can see inside.

"Are you ready to go?" I hear Dee ask, tone a little too fucking happy for so early in the morning. It sounds a little smug, too. "Or are you two both staying to enjoy the honeymoon?"

"What?" Renny asks him, sounding just like I feel, grumpy, tired and a little bit horny.

Okay, maybe the horny bit is just me, but I can't help it when he's walking around like *that*.

"You don't remember what happened last night?" Dee asks, quiet for a few moments before he starts laughing.

Hard.

He pushes the door open and steps inside, Renny locking it behind him with a harsh curse.

"Mrs. Steel," he says to me, smile wider than I've ever seen it. "How are you this morning? You don't seem to be glowing. Did Renegade here not blow your mind with his bedroom skills?"

Renny slaps him on the back of his head, which I really appreciate, until I start processing what he is saying.

We're in Vegas.

Honeymoon?

Mrs. Steel?

I think we all know what he's getting at here, but no, just fucking no. There is no way I would do that. I rack my memory, flashing back to every place we went, every club and every bar, every laugh. I remember doing Fireball shots with Renny, and then I remember…

Nothing.

What happened after the Fireballs at Hakkasan?

We share a look, and he looks just as concerned as I feel.

I glance down at my hand and see a wedding band. One that wasn't there yesterday. Dread fills me.

I eye Renny's hand and see a plain gold band on his.

Fuck.

Renny studies me for a moment, then shakes his head. "No. I don't know what fucking *Punk'd* shit you're trying to pull on me, Dee, but we drank, we danced, and then we fucking came back to this hotel room, where I was a gentleman and slept on the floor."

"Since when are you a gentleman—"

"Dee, what the fuck," Renny growls, crossing his arms over his chest.

Dee hands him his phone. Renny stares at the screen, and I jump out of bed and rush over to him, needing to see this, especially after hearing my obnoxious laughter blazing through the speaker.

I'm silent as I watch me, in my clothes from last night, standing opposite Renny, holding his hands and staring into his eyes.

"Fuck," I whisper as it all comes back to me.

"I'm having so much fun!" I say, smiling widely. I'm clearly very drunk, but I haven't had this much fun in a while. "I can't believe you've been so close to me this entire time and we've never hung out."

"I know," he replies, stirring the ice in his drink. "I knew you were beautiful, but I had no idea you'd be like this..."

"Like what?" I ask him, leaning closer to him, my chin resting on my palm.

"Funny," he says, scanning my eyes. "Smart. Witty. I don't know, just different."

"You like me," I reply with a smug grin. "I'm glad my car broke down, you know that? We wouldn't be here right now if it didn't."

Renny reaches his hand out and cups my face, my own hand dropping away. When he leans closer to kiss me, I don't stop him. Instead, I all but jump onto his lap and kiss him deeper, pressing my body against his, holding on

*for dear life and enjoying the ride. My heart races, and
when he pulls away I can't help but smile against his lips.*

"Yeah, you really like me," I say, smiling, my heavily
lidded eyes locked with his.

Wincing, I cover my face with my hands, remembering
how bold I was, and the fact that I didn't care who was
watching is a testament to how much I'd been drinking,
because I'm usually not one for public displays of affection. More flashbacks hit me as I remember exactly how
I got myself into this predicament.

*Stopping in front of a wedding chapel, I stare up at the
sign. Renny stops ahead of me, turning to see why I'm
no longer next to him.*

*"What are you doing?" he asks, walking back over to
me. "We need to get back to the hotel."*

*"Do you know what would be a great idea?" I ask,
sighing happily. "If we proved just how perfect we are
for each other."*

*Mind buzzing, I'm clearly not thinking straight by this
point.*

*Pulling at Renny's arm, I glance up at him. "You said
you'd show me a true Vegas experience."*

*"I did say that, didn't I," he murmurs, staring down at
me and grinning. "We need rings. We can't do this without rings. And we need my brothers here. It isn't a wedding without the Knights."*

*"All we need is each other," I slur, laughing to myself.
"But yeah, we also need those things."*

What the fuck.

Dee takes his phone back, and then takes a picture of

both of our expressions. "I wish you could see your faces right now," he chuckles, and then presses a few buttons on his phone. "Everyone is going to lose their shit when they see this."

I'm speechless, my mind racing, not knowing how the fuck I have managed to get myself into this situation. Last night I messaged my sister and told her the new plan, that I would be staying here one more night to have a little fun, but there's no way in hell I'm going to tell her about this clusterfuck.

I'm just going to fix this and bury it under the rug, along with memories of the douche lord I lost my virginity to, the fact that I have my ex's name tattooed on my ass and any other generally bad decisions I've made over the years.

Not knowing what to do or how to react to this, I decide to blame the only other person I can. Pointing a finger at Renny's chest, I narrow my eyes and scowl. "This is all your fault."

He rubs the back of his neck. "You just saw the same video as I did. You weren't exactly saying no."

Opening my mouth, and then closing it, I step away from him and puff out a tired breath. "It's fine. We can get it annulled, we didn't even consummate the marriage." I pause and then add, "Did we?"

"Not that I know of," he groans, pushing Dee toward the door. The bastard is still laughing like a fucking hyena. "What time are we leaving?"

"We're waiting for you two," Dee admits. "I'll tell them you'll be ready in thirty? Or do you need longer?"

I'm going to need longer.

"Thirty is fine," Renny grumbles, closing the door on him.

I've got a change of clothes that I luckily shoved in my handbag, and I've never been more grateful to have planned for the unexpected.

"I need to have a shower," I state, moving past him and into the bathroom. When I close the door, I lean my back on it and close my eyes. I can't believe I allowed something like this to happen, and I can't remember the last time I was so reckless.

After stripping down and having a scalding hot shower, wishing it would wash away my sins, I realize I left my bag on the bed and now I have to exit the bathroom in nothing but a towel. I open the door and stick my head out, seeing Renny sitting on the bed with his face in his hands, probably having the same mental lecture I just gave myself in the shower.

"Can you pass me my bag?" I ask him in a soft tone.

He lifts his head and takes me in before standing, picking up my bag and bringing it to me. He looks tired, which is understandable, but I hope that he's going to be okay to ride.

"Do you want to rest? We don't have to leave with everyone else if you're not up for it," I say, taking my bag from his hands and lingering.

"I'm fine," he says. "We slept for seven hours, it's already lunchtime. I'll just get us something to eat before we head off. How are you feeling?"

"In general, or about the whole being a walking cliché and getting drunkenly married in Vegas thing?" I ask in a dry tone, hiking up my towel.

"Both." He grimaces, running his hand through his hair in frustration. "I don't know, tell me what you need from me right now. I'm not good at this shit, so you need to tell me."

I'm not sure what he's asking me exactly, but it sounds like he wants me to tell him what to do to fix this, and to make it all okay. I think the only thing we can do is get our asses home and get an annulment, or whatever we need to do to get unmarried. I'm too hungover to even try to attempt to fix this right now. I just want to get home, survive this bike ride and collapse onto my bed in a pile of relief and regret. What's done is done, and no matter how much we want an instant fix, there's nothing we can do. There's no point stressing about it. It won't help the situation.

"You already trying to work on your communication skills for me, husband," I tease, trying to make light of the situation. "Next you'll be compromising."

He starts laughing then, and I join in.

Sometimes, it's either laugh, or cry.

Chapter Eight

"Do you think after one night he's going to lose fifty percent of his assets?" I hear Dee ask Temper as he puts gas in his bike. Temper simply shakes his head in annoyance. "Renny, say goodbye to your second Harley!"

"Dee, you need to shut the fuck up," Renny replies, gritting his teeth. Dee just laughs; the man must have a death wish.

Temper hasn't said much about the whole thing, and I wonder what's going on in that mind of his. I don't know why, but he's not someone I want to disappoint, and I feel like I haven't really shown him and everyone else the best version of myself on this trip.

"Is Temper angry about what happened?" I ask Renny as he pumps gas into his own bike. "He's been even quieter than usual."

Not that I've spent a lot of time with him, but on the ride here and on our night out, he was a little more open and chatty. Just a little. I don't think he's the overly friendly type.

"No one is angry at you," Renny assures me, frowning. "But that doesn't mean that they're not going to give us shit from now until the end of time."

"Your assets are safe," I promise, smirking. "I'm the

last woman you need to worry about that stuff with. I'm too proud to take anything from a man, or anything I haven't earned myself."

Not to mention with only one night of marriage, I hardly doubt that would hold up in court.

"I know," he murmurs. "Don't listen to Dee. He's an asshole, and he loves to stir up shit. I'm not worried about any of that. I'm just a little pissed because I planned on asking you out on a proper date when we got home, but after this bullshit, you're probably going to run home and never look back."

My eyes widen at his honesty. "You were going to ask me out?"

I don't know why I'm surprised, but I am. There is definitely something between us, I'm not too blind to feel and see that, but we live completely different lives and I don't know if I fit in with his. Yeah, we kissed last night, but we were completely intoxicated, and if we weren't we might have been smarter about the whole thing and not given in to temptation.

Sometimes, the best decision is to walk away instead of getting involved with someone, especially when you know that in the end, it's just not going to work out. If my mom had done that, it might have saved her a world of pain.

And I'm not volunteering myself for any heartbreak.

Been there and done that.

He nods slowly. "Why do you sound surprised? You're beautiful, smart and funny, and you never complain or ask for anything. Not to mention I've been checking you out since the day you moved in."

"I hope you added that line in your vows," I joke, feeling my face heat. "Not that either of us would remember."

I hope no one else remembers either.

Renny studies me for a few seconds, not missing my deflection. "Can I take you out on a proper date one night this week?"

Fuck, he knows how to put me on the spot, doesn't he?

"Well, we are married now, so I guess it's the least we can do," I say, once again using humor as a defense mechanism.

"Izzy—"

"I do like you, Renny," I blurt out, glancing out at the road. "But can we talk about this when we make it home?"

With everything that has happened, my emotions are all over the place.

I also can't think straight when I'm around him. It's like he turns me into this other person and I don't know if that's a good thing or not. He brings out the life in me, but that isn't always the safest way to live. He's also way too good-looking, and yes, that's a thing. Everyone knows you can't trust a man who looks that good. I mean, look at Merve. I just told Renny I like him, laying all my cards out, like I usually do. I was never good at bluffing, but I don't want to play games either.

I do like him.

But this is all a bit much right now.

"Yeah, of course," he replies, brows furrowing. "Do you want me to get you anything? More water? Snacks?"

"No, I'm okay. Thank you." I force a smile.

He's been nothing but a gentleman, and it's not only his fault how this entire thing played out, so I can't hold it against him. It takes two to tango, or two to get married in this case, and I saw the video—no one was holding a gun to my head. In fact, my face screamed *I've won the man lotto!*

I cringe just thinking about it.

"Okay, let me know if you want to stop again," he says, and then we're off.

Riding hungover has to be one of the worst experiences of my life, and all I have to do is hold on for dear life. It's Renny who has to concentrate and make sure that we stay safe.

I rest my cheek against the warm leather of his cut and take a few deep breaths.

I can do this.

Without throwing up on him.

We finally make it home, and when my eyes land on my house I'm so relieved, I almost cry. Renny helps me off the bike and I remove my helmet and hand it back to him.

"Thank you so much for everything," I tell him, staring directly into his eyes. "You saved my ass by getting me to my sister, and I really appreciate it."

"What are husbands for?" he says, then grimaces and rubs the back of his neck. "But seriously, it was no problem at all. I was happy to help. I guess I'll see you around?"

I nod. "Yep, I guess so."

Especially considering we have to get an annulment.

"Bye, Renny," I say, giving him a little wave and then turning toward my door. I'm safely inside when I hear the rumble of his engine driving off. After I message Ariel to let her know that I'm home, I take a long shower and drink a lot of water before jumping into my bed and lying there, enjoying being home.

Ever since I got on Renny's bike, my life has been turned upside down, and it's going to take a little time to process everything.

When I fall asleep, though, I dream about him, and if that doesn't mean something, I don't know what does.

"Hey," I say, opening the door and smiling at him. "How are you?"

"Good," Renny replies, dangling my car keys in front of him. "I brought your car back."

I've spent the last few days catching up on work and life in general, and I've barely even left my house. Mostly because I haven't had my car.

"Thank you. How much do I owe you?" I ask, stepping outside to have a look at the car.

"Nothing," he says. "She should run smoothly from now on, but let me know if you have any more issues."

"What do you mean, nothing?" I ask, frowning. I've always paid my own way, and that's not going to stop now. "Will you please let me pay you? I don't want you to be out of pocket for me."

Brown eyes pin me to my spot. "You owe me nothing, Izzy. Don't worry about it, it didn't cost a lot, and I promise you my bank account won't even notice."

I roll my eyes. "That's not the point." I take a breath, pause and then add, "Seriously, thank you, Renny. I mean it."

"It's not a big deal," he replies, waving it off.

But he's wrong. It *is* a big deal. These days it's rare to find people that are willing to help others without asking for anything in return.

"I owe you one," I tell him quietly, glancing over at him. "I mean it."

"Stop it," he replies, placing the keys in my hand and closing my fingers around them. "I almost forgot," he adds, opening the passenger door and pulling out a brown bag and a coffee. "I brought you something."

"Aren't you the gift that keeps on giving?" I grin, shaking my head. "What have you brought me?"

"Just something to keep you going while you work," he murmurs, scanning my outfit. "Is this your work uniform?"

I glance down at my very well-worn and loved Harry Potter pajamas and then back up at him. "This is me looking fancy." His lip twitches as I take the goods from him. "Would you like to come in?"

"I'd love to."

As he steps inside and closer to me, his familiar scent hits my nostrils and makes me want to rub myself against him. I don't, of course, because that would be weird. And probably be considered assault.

"Cool place you have," he says as he wanders into my domain.

"Thanks. It's my little slice of heaven," I admit, leading him into my living room where the TV is still on, and my laptop is sitting upright on the black leather couch. "And this is where I work. Or sometimes I work in bed. I like to mix things up every now and again."

"You don't have an actual office?" he asks, brow furrowing as he sits down on the couch. He takes up so much space in my house, but I don't know if that's because he's such a commanding presence or because my place is too small to accommodate his big frame.

"I do, but I don't really use it," I say, sitting down and opening the bag to see what he brought me.

"A bagel and doughnuts," he says, watching me.

"You remembered." I had told him before we left that

bagels and doughnuts were two of my favorite foods. The fact that he remembered means a lot.

He listened and took note.

I didn't know men like that really existed.

"I remember everything you say," he says with a shrug. "I made sure they put extra cream cheese, too."

"I'm impressed, Renny, I'm not going to lie."

He smirks, and then eyes my laptop screen. "What are you working on today?"

"A company wants me to design a new logo for them, in addition to coming up with a whole new promotional package. So I'm working on that, and some brochures and flyers for them," I explain. "What about you? What do you have on the agenda today?"

"The Knights run a few businesses, and one is a bike shop we just opened. We sell custom bikes, that sort of thing, so I'm working in there today."

Interesting. I've wondered how a motorcycle club like them makes money without doing something illegal.

"Custom bikes, that sounds pretty cool," I say, breaking my bagel and offering him the bigger half.

He takes it, our fingers touching in the exchange. "Yeah, it only just opened, so I'm going to be spending a lot of time there, getting the business on its feet." He takes a big bite and moans. "Fuck, this is actually pretty good. It's been years since I've had one of these."

"Told you." I grin.

"Everyone has been asking when you're going to come over and say hello, so this is me officially inviting you over to the clubhouse for drinks and dinner tomorrow night," he says, licking cream cheese off his finger, brown eyes pinned on me.

That takes me by surprise. I never thought I'd ever

go to the clubhouse. But I did have a good time with the guys in Vegas, despite getting married. Uh, yes, I keep forgetting that I'm married to Renny. I guess I should get to know his family.

"I guess I can do that," I find myself agreeing. "What time do you want me over?"

"I'll come get you at like seven, if that works for you?" he suggests.

"It's a two-minute walk. I think I can manage getting there without getting lost," I say, rolling my eyes.

He barks out a laugh. "I know you can manage, but I don't want you walking around alone in the dark."

He stands up and flashes me a smile, like it's all sorted then, even though I didn't agree, and heads to my front door, making a quick exit.

It's only after he's gone that I realize we didn't even discuss getting our annulment. After calling two lawyers and playing phone tag with them, I need to find out where he is on the whole situation so I know what I have to do to move the process along.

We obviously can't just stay married, can we?

Chapter Nine

Wrapping my trench coat around myself, I'm glad I wore jeans tonight as the evening chill hits me. I walk through the vacant land toward the clubhouse. I don't like being told what to do, and if I want to walk myself down the damn street, I'm going to do just that.

I can hear the music before I can see the brown brick building, and I don't miss the extra bikes out front. I have no idea what to expect tonight, but after spending some time with Renny, Temper, Saint and Dee, I don't feel too nervous. If I want to leave, I can at any time, and I know without a doubt that Renny will make sure I'm kept safe.

Safe from anyone except him, that is.

Renegade. What the hell am I going to do with him?

"Izzy?" I hear him call from the open metal fence. "I told you I was going to come and get you!"

He looks good. Black leather boots, black ripped jeans and a black V-neck T-shirt, tattoos covering all of his skin barring his neck and face, and a scowl that should intimidate me, but doesn't.

"And I said I'd be fine walking," I say as he approaches. "And see, I made it alive. All on my own."

"Smartass," he mutters, but grins and offers me his hand. "Come on, let me give you the grand tour."

We pass a few men who nod in our direction, and then enter the large building through a wooden door. "This place is bigger than I thought," I admit.

"There's plenty of space," he agrees. "The backyard is huge, and that's where you'll usually find us. Bedrooms are down there." He points down a hallway. "And the kitchen is through there," he says as he points to a door in the other direction.

The place is surprisingly neat, rustic and has a very bachelor feel to it, but I don't not like it. It has ample space, like he said, and a cool vibe to it.

"Do you want something to drink?" he asks, laughing when I instantly shake my head.

"No thank you, I'm only just getting over that hangover, and the last thing I want is more alcohol. I think I'm going to be sober for the next few months, at least."

"We do have nonalcoholic options," he suggests, handing me a can of soda. "I'm with you, actually. I'm not drinking tonight."

I don't think we could make any worse decisions than last time, but I don't want to test that theory. I just want to hang out with Renny, with my wits about me, and I'm a person who can still have fun without drinking.

"Hey, look who it is!" Dee calls out, coming over and giving me a quick hug. "Welcome."

"Thank you for having me," I say, smiling when I see Skylar coming over.

"Hey, Izzy," she says, pulling me into a warm hug. "Nice to officially meet you, and on much better terms this time. How have you been?"

"Good, and yourself?" I ask her, studying the beautiful woman. With her sharp green eyes and stunning red hair, I don't know who is luckier, her or Saint.

"I'm great. I hear that you tied the knot with a Knight, which means you're family now," she snickers, pulling me aside from the men. "I need to hear the entire story from you, because I know men like to leave shit out." She leads me inside to the kitchen and pulls out a chair for me. "Tell me everything."

"Well," I start, unprepared for this interrogation. "We thought having one night out would be a good idea, because I've never had a wild night out in Vegas, and one thing led to another. We all ended up drinking copious amounts of alcohol, and at some point in the night we walked past a chapel and thought tying the knot was a wonderful idea."

"Man, you must have been seriously wasted," she says, eyes wide.

"Enough that I only remember snippets of the night, and if I didn't see the video footage with my own eyes, probably wouldn't even believe that we were that stupid," I admit, cringing. "This is so out of character for me, I don't even know what to think at this point."

I don't really make rash decisions normally, and I don't usually do spontaneous. I don't know what came over me that night, but no one is more surprised than me.

"So what's going to happen now? Everyone has been giving Renny so much shit, but he hasn't really said much. And you're here now, so does that mean—"

"We aren't going to stay married, no."

"But—"

"I don't even know him," I whisper-yell, shaking my head. "I'm waiting to hear back from a few attorneys that I called. I have no idea how I got here," I admit, covering my face with my hands.

"It's not that bad," she assures me, reaching out to

touch my arm. "We're here for you, and we know a great lawyer that can help get it sorted out. Have you heard of Bentley & Channing Law Firm? We can give them a call. I'm sure it's something that can be sorted out fairly easily."

I have heard of them before, or at least I've seen their advertisements on TV and social media, but I didn't call them because I know they are largely out of my price range. I called a few local, smaller law firms and I can't even get a call back from those ones.

"I hope so," I say, frowning.

"It will be sorted," she promises. "But are you sure that's what you want to do?"

I move my hand away from my eyes and look at her. "Yes, I'm sure. I know Renny is a very sexy man, but if I ever get married let's just say I want a cuter, more romantic story to tell instead of we got drunk and couldn't remember getting married, but we did it anyway. That screams more that we are irresponsible alcoholics rather than cute and romantic."

Skylar laughs, her shoulders shaking. "You're hilarious. You're gonna fit in here so easily. And I'm happy to have another woman around the place, because the sausage fest is getting old."

I almost choke on my mouthful of soda.

She just grins. "What? It's true."

"Tell me about him," I say, wanting to learn all that I can about my current husband.

"I know that he's been a member ever since he turned eighteen," she starts, running her index finger along her bottom lip. "Saint trusts him with his life. The MC is his family. He's always been a bit of a joker, and somewhat distant if I'm being honest. Still waters run deep. I think that you're going to see a side of him that none of us have," she says like she's contemplating something. "Oh, and he's had a crush on you since you moved in. At least that's what I've heard."

I smile at her last comment. "I've never met anyone like him," I admit, considering her words. The man definitely lives and breathes the MC, something that will have a huge impact on us if we progress into something.

"Renny is a good man though, that I can promise you," she continues, looking me in the eye. "I trust him completely."

I don't admit that I already agree. "Well, I suppose that's good considering he's my—"

I glance out the window, and see something that makes any humor slide away from my face. "Who is that sitting next to my husband?"

Skylar lifts her head to look in my line of sight. "I don't know. Want to go out and find out?"

I do, and I don't.

He's not mine, I mean, I guess he is legally, for now, but he's not really mine. Still...

"Yeah, let's go out there," I decide. Whether he's mine or not, he invited me here tonight, and there's no way in hell I'm hanging around if he's going to be sitting there and flirting with other women in front of me. We both stand up and head back outside, which has now filled up with more people, laughter and chatting almost overpowering the music.

I sit down right across from Renny, who smiles with his eyes as they land on me. He puts his phone away, as if to give me his full attention. I check out his new friend, who is chattering away, and arch my brow at him. Skylar sits down next to me and stares at him, having my back.

Renny looks confused for a second, but then glances next to him, eyes widening with realization. He instantly shakes his head. "Seriously? You think I'm going to flirt with a woman in front of the woman I want and am trying to impress?" he asks me, lip twitching. "I've got balls, Izzy, but I'm not that stupid." He looks to the woman next to him. "This is…uhhh."

"Bec," she inserts, frowning. "I was just introducing myself to all the men."

"I bet you were," Skylar says, rolling her eyes. "Renny is married. See that ring on his finger?"

I'm surprised that he's still wearing the ring, considering that I took mine off when we got back here. Maybe he hasn't really thought about it, or maybe he's just owning it to his friends.

"I was just saying hello," Bec backtracks, placing her hands up in surrender. She stands and then walks away, sitting down next to Dee instead. Much safer territory.

"Never pictured you as the jealous type," Renny mutters, unable to wipe the grin away from his face. "I kind of like it."

"I wasn't jealous," I assure him. "I just wanted to make sure my hubby wasn't out here making me look stupid by entertaining some other woman."

His expression sobers at that comment, and he leans forward and takes my hand in his. "I only have eyes for you, Izzy. I'm not here to waste anyone's time. I'm too old for that shit, all right? Women are easy to find, but women like you? They're rare. You are rare. And you wouldn't be here right now, around my family, if that didn't mean something to me. I know we don't know each other well yet, so I'm going with my gut here, and just from what I've seen from you so far. I'm trusting that you're being as genuine as I think you are."

Swallowing hard, I nod, feeling a little sheepish, and lift my soda up at him. "To you not being stupid."

Skylar laughs out loud. "I love this girl already."

"Hopefully she sticks around," Renny replies, eyes locked on mine.

I wasn't planning on it, but I keep getting in deeper and deeper with this man. I'm so attracted to him, but it's more than that. He intrigues me, and the more I learn the more I want to know.

"Well, I'm here, aren't I?" I remind him, smiling at Saint when he comes over and pulls Skylar onto his lap.

"What have I missed?" he asks, nuzzling her neck.

"Nothing much, just the cutest interaction with a woman I've ever seen Renny have," she says, sighing heavily. "You two are super sweet."

"Never thought I'd hear the words *Renny* and *cute* in the same sentence," Saint mutters, looking over at his friend and slapping him on the back. "Another one bites the dust, hey, brother."

"And they got married before us," Skylar points out, frowning. "You need to up your game, Saint."

Saint cups her face and kisses her. I don't know if it's to shut her up or what, but it works. "Our time will come. For now let the newlyweds have their moment."

I can only imagine how much grief the MC must have been giving Renny, but he seems to take it well. Or at least he does when I'm around. Who knows what he's thinking and saying when I'm not?

I never thought that I'd be one to have trust issues, but with the dating scene how it is and with Renny being so good-looking, and a biker… I don't know, it's just a little hard to believe that he's all for me. I don't even have low self-esteem or anything like that. It's just my brain working overtime, not wanting to get hurt or to be made a fool of.

I know that love doesn't work like that, and I need to be in it to win it, so to speak. I need to put myself out there and hope I made the right choice in Renny. I didn't even realize until this moment that I actually wanted to try to make a relationship with him work. Over the last few days I did a lot of overthinking and told myself that nothing else was going to happen between us, but the second he comes to my house and invites me over, here I am.

"So where are we going on our honeymoon, hubby? I've always wanted to go to Croatia," I tease, taking a sip of my drink and staring up at him.

Saint barks out a laugh. "When you're married to someone on probation, I think the only places you can travel to are within the country, Izzy."

What?

Well, shit.

Chapter Ten

"I think this is how we got into this mess in the first place," I laugh, letting Renny spin me around and dance against me. Hours later and the party is still in full swing, and I'm having a great night. "I'm having flashbacks."

"I think you might be right," he says into my ear, hands on my waist, my back pressed against his hard chest. "It's not my fault that you're such a good dancer."

"You're not so bad yourself, but you already know that, don't you?" I say coyly, raising my arms above my head and behind me, so that I'm holding on to the back of his neck. "It's nice to see that we're still like this without the aid of liquid courage."

He chuckles. "That wasn't even a concern for me. I was just worried the whole thing scared you off, because I don't think you're usually the reckless type, which makes me the bad influence."

"You are right there," I say, spinning around to face him. "You're definitely the bad influence in this marriage."

He smirks and softly cups my cheek. "Never gets old saying that, does it? Never thought I'd get married at all, never mind this week."

"Why not?" I ask him, curious. "Not the commitment type?"

"No, I don't think it was that. I can definitely commit, for the right woman, and be loyal and all of that. I guess it's just been a long-ass time since someone piqued my interest, so I was losing hope."

"Yeah, I'm sure you were sobbing, alone," I mutter, rolling my eyes. "Don't play innocent, Renegade, it doesn't suit you."

His smirk grows. "Never claimed I was innocent. However, there is a deeper side to me, if you look through all the bullshit."

"Buried deep in there, is it?" I ask, tone laced with humor.

"Very deep, just how I like it," he whispers into my ear, pulls back and winks at me.

I shake my head. "You're something else, you know that?"

"Hey, you married me," he reminds me, not for the first time. "Not that we were coherent, but you know…"

"Skylar was saying you guys know some top lawyers that can sort our little situation out."

He places my hand over his heart. "Ouch. So desperate to get rid of me? That hurts, Izzy."

"Not as much as it's going to hurt if my sister finds out what happened," I groan, wincing at the thought. "We'll both be dead. She won't care if I'm her baby sister and you're a badass biker, we're both going down."

"One problem at a time," he says. "Look, I know the situation isn't ideal and I'll speak to a lawyer about sorting our shit out this week."

"Thank you."

"But I want to keep seeing you," he continues. "What are you doing tomorrow night? How about we go out for dinner?"

"Okay," I reply without hesitation.

"Okay?" He actually sounds surprised, which is endearing.

I nod. "Yeah, okay. Why, do you want me to put up a fight or something? Trust me, I considered it. But I like you, too, okay, and there's no point fucking around and pretending I don't. Our story isn't starting off in the traditional sense…"

But no true love story ever is.

He flashes his straight, white teeth at me. "You won't regret it."

"Famous last words," I reply, laughing as he dips me back, my hair flowing and almost touching the ground.

Apparently I'm a little more flexible than I thought I was.

We have something to eat, and I chat about nothing and everything with Skylar and the rest of the men.

"I basically grew up in the clubhouse," Skylar tells me, explaining how she ended up here with Saint. "My mom used to be the former president's—" her face crumbles a bit "—old lady. Hammer was the only dad I've ever known, but I moved away when I was in my teens. He passed away last year. And then Temper took over."

I don't miss the flash of pain in her eyes that she quickly tries to mask.

"I'm sorry to hear that," I say, ducking my head. "I know what it's like to lose a parent, and yeah…" Tears prickle my eyes as I think of my mom. "It's the worst thing anyone can go through."

When I lift my eyes Skylar smiles sadly at me. "I'm sorry that we share that."

"Me, too," I whisper. "So how did you connect with Saint?"

"Well, Mom moved me away for a few years and I had no contact with the MC or my dad, until Saint wrote me a letter." She pauses, and then adds, "From prison, actually."

Skylar mentioning prison reminds me about Renny being on parole—something I haven't asked him about yet.

"Why did you lose contact with them?" I ask her, brow furrowing.

"Mom didn't want me to have anything to do with them," she admits, lips tightening. "It's a long and complicated story, but when Hammer broke up with her, she didn't want them to have any contact with me, either. But I came back and fell in love with Saint, who I had the biggest crush on as a teenager, and the rest is history."

"That's quite the story," I tell her, eyes widening and processing everything Skylar has been through.

"Ever think you'd be here?" Temper asks me as he sits down, catching the end of the conversation. I noticed that he's been nursing his one beer all night. Maybe he's not much of a drinker, but I don't miss the fact that he's always scanning the group, as if making sure everything is okay. I know he's the president of the MC, but is this what being president means? Always being on alert, always watching. I wonder if he ever takes a break.

"No," I admit, leaning back and studying him. "I'd hear the music from afar, but never once did I think I'd be inside these walls. It's a whole different world over here."

"Feel free to bring all of your hot friends over," Dee says as he walks over, winking. "You know what they say, the more the merrier."

"I don't know if that counts for STDs," I fire back, making everyone laugh.

Dee's jaw drops open, and then he bursts out laughing, too. "And I thought you were a nice girl."

"I am, but not too nice. I don't think I could survive here if I wasn't."

More laughter, but I'm being dead serious. The men love to tease and joke. But I'm learning that anyone who is overly sensitive wouldn't last here, not to mention that I feel like everyone in here can sense weakness. The men are all strong, and I've only met Skylar, but I can tell she is, too.

"Ain't that the truth," Renny agrees, studying me. "We've all been through a lot here, and our brotherhood comes with a price."

"And what price is that?" I ask unwaveringly, but I already know.

Trouble.

That's the price.

These men aren't saints even though one of them is named such, and I can only imagine the type of things they have to deal with on a daily basis. Yet when I sit here with all of them, I don't feel scared, or worried. I just feel like I'm hanging out with a bunch of friends. I feel safe, at least with Renny next to me, and I know that he will do anything to protect me.

I've never felt that with any man before, my father included.

I've never had a boyfriend I just knew would jump in front of a bullet for me, one I could trust infinitely. Hell, other than my sister, I don't have anyone I would trust on that level. It's a powerful feeling, and it gives me strength.

Although being around the MC would mean that my chances of getting hurt or being put in danger increase drastically, I can't help but like being here.

Maybe that makes me crazy, but it also makes me feel alive.

And for someone like me, who simply breezes through life being as closed off as I can, that is *huge*.

"Where do I start?" Renny asks, touching the stubble on his cheek with his palm. "Any time one of us has a problem, it becomes all of our problems, so let's just say we deal with a lot of shit on a daily basis."

"You trying to scare me off now, Renny?" I ask, arching my brow. "I thought you brought me here tonight to try and make me give you a real chance."

"She's bold," Dee mutters, shaking his head. "Fuckin' bold."

"Just letting you know what you're getting into," Renny says, pushing my hair back behind my ear. "So you can't say that I didn't warn you further down the line."

"Warning noted," I reply, looking around at the group. "How about the rest of you? Have any other warnings for me?"

"Yeah, Renny snores," Temper informs me, eyes filled with amusement. "And he's the main reason we have to get a fuckin' cleaning service coming in, because when he cooks, he trashes the whole kitchen."

"But he does cook, right?" I ask, sounding hopeful to even my own ears.

"I can cook," he assures me, laughing softly. "Is that important to you?"

"Well, I like to eat," I reply with a shrug. "And yeah, it's kind of sexy when a man knows his way around a kitchen."

And a clitoris, but I'll save that one for another time.

"Maybe I should cook for you tomorrow night then,"

he says so only I can hear. "Blow you away with my skills."

That actually does sound kind of nice, and a little more personal than just going out for dinner. "Okay, sounds good. There was actually something I wanted to ask you."

"What is it?"

"Well, it was mentioned that you were on parole. Care to clear that up for me?" I ask, studying him.

He licks his lips before he speaks. "I *am* on parole, but only for another few months."

"He got into a fight," Dee adds, shrugging like it happens every day. "For assault."

My eyes widen.

"They started it," Renny grumbles, watching me.

"They?"

"Yeah, there were three of them, and somehow I'm the one who was arrested for it," he replies, scowling.

"So three against one and somehow you're the bad guy?" I ask, frowning.

"I'm a Knight," is all he replies. "Goes with the territory."

I know these men aren't all sugar and spice, but that sounds kind of unfair. I guess when you're in this world and your reputation precedes you, it does go with the territory. However, never in my wildest dreams did I imagine I'd be married to someone who has any kind of criminal record.

Renny did try to warn me away, so I'm not going into this blind.

The messed-up part? Despite the revelation, all I can think about is our date, and whether he is going to cook for me here, with everyone around. That wouldn't exactly be romantic, and I imagine everyone will also want to eat, so it wouldn't exactly be a date. Still, it's his date to plan, so I don't say anything.

Hopefully he thinks things through, especially if his aim truly is to blow me away.

Renny walks me back home around midnight, and even though the party is nowhere near being over, it was time for me to leave and get some sleep.

"I didn't realize how loud our music is until right now," he admits as I search in my handbag for my house keys. "I'm surprised you haven't called the cops in the past."

"It doesn't bother me," I say, opening the door. "Would you like to come in, or do you have to get back to the party?"

"I can come in," he murmurs, stepping inside with me and closing the door behind him.

I know I shouldn't have invited him in, but I guess I'm not ready to say goodbye just yet. "I'm going to make coffee. Do you want one?"

"I'd love one," he says, following me into the kitchen and sitting down on my wooden barstool. "Being the only sober people at a party requires a lot of patience."

"It does, but at least we will remember everything that everyone did and said and can give them shit about it tomorrow," I say, grinning. "It's one of my favorite things to do."

"You're evil," he states, eyes flashing with approval. "I knew I liked you for a reason. Well, other than your good looks, kindness and intelligence…"

"How do you know I'm kind and intelligent?" I ask, arching my brow in challenge.

"Well, let's see, you dropped everything and ran to help your sister, the way you speak about people, the kindness in your eyes… I could go on. And intelligence? Again, the way you speak. The fact that you run your own business means you must be talented. And before you ask, I Googled you so I've seen your website and images of some of the work you have done. Temper even said we should ask you to design a new MC logo for us."

My eyes widen at his reply. Not only is he extremely observant, but he looked me up. While it could be considered a bit stalkerish, who hasn't Googled someone they've dated? "You're a little bit cute, you know that?"

"I do now," he whispers, coming up behind me and wrapping his arms around me. "I don't know what the fuck you've done to me, girl."

"I've done nothing."

Yet. And that word lingers between us.

Turning around I lift up on my tiptoes as he lowers his face, our lips close but not touching. This is that point, the one that I won't be able to come back from.

I make the first move.

Pressing my lips against his, my eyes flutter closed as we kiss. I know we kissed that night in Vegas, but for me, this counts as our first official kiss, because that whole night is a blur. As my heart begins to race, I know it's one I'm never going to regret.

He cups the back of my neck and takes control of the kiss, his soft lips mastering mine, his tongue gently dancing with mine.

My head starts to feel dizzy, lost in his taste, scent and touch, and when he pulls away with those brown eyes looking into my soul… I know that I'm in big fucking trouble.

"You're so beautiful," he murmurs, scanning my face.

"I better let you get some sleep. Big day in the office to-morrow?"

"Something like that." I grin, leaning into him and resting my cheek against his chest. "You smell good. I wanted to tell you that all night."

"Why didn't you?" he asks, tone amused. "I guess I wanted to tell you that you looked stunning all night, but I didn't either."

"Really? I was the most clothed person there," I point out, laughing.

"And still the most attractive," he replies, kissing the top of my head. "I don't know. I guess we're both still testing the waters with each other because we don't know where we stand. It's not the easiest of positions to be in. I mean, we're technically married, but not actually together. And I don't really know what the fuck I'm supposed to be doing. I know what I want, but you kind of need to be on board with that, too. We both need to actually communicate with each other and tell each other what we want, up front, no fucking around."

"I know what you mean. I never thought of it like that, but you're right."

Married but not together. Now I understand why people are so into that show *Married at First Sight*. I always thought it was the lamest idea. But now I'm proof that maybe, just maybe, there is something to it.

I laugh internally—I sound like an idiot.

And he's also right about our communication. I think we've both tried to let our actions do the talking, but we both are kind of unsure on where the other is at, because no one has straight out said what they are feeling.

"I want you," he declares. "And this is me telling you,

no mixed signals, no nothing. I want to try to see if this can be something."

"I want that, too," I reply, swallowing. "And I have to be honest, I'm not the best at talking out my feelings or giving compliments. I'll think them but sometimes won't say anything, almost like I'm a little shy to. It's something I'm trying to work on," I admit.

My ex-boyfriend Leo always said that I never said nice things about him. I thought he was ridiculous and that he just wanted me to stroke his ego, which I wasn't going to do. But I've realized that I could have been more complimentary. Everyone likes to hear that they are doing well or that they are attractive, and I know that now.

I have to remind myself to do it, though. I'm lost in my own head a lot, and sometimes it's hard for me to be present. I think this is because I don't feel like I need many compliments. I mean, they are nice to hear, but I don't need them. Mom complimented me like any doting parent would, but my dad never did, always pushing us to do better and achieve more. Like nothing was ever good enough. As a result, I taught myself that I never needed to hear praise, which I think made me stronger. But as an indirect result, I in turn never give compliments either.

"You have a shy side?" he jokes, eyes smiling. "No, I know what you mean. Everyone has little issues with communication, but if you know what they are then you're already ahead of most people. I know that when I get angry I tend to just walk away to calm down instead of talking it out, which a lot of women don't like. But I prefer to have a clear head before I have a proper conversation, or who knows what the fuck will come out of my mouth."

"That's probably a blessing in disguise then." I grin,

reaching up to touch his leather cut. "I have a lot of pride, and I know it's supposed to be a good thing, but I can tell you now that it's a flaw. Add being stubborn and I'm not always the easiest person to be around."

"Sounds like you're warning me now."

"Well, now you can't tell me that I didn't warn you," I reply, winking at him.

He smiles and kisses me again, and then I'm smiling against his lips in return, and all is right in the world.

After we linger for the next hour or so, I walk him to the door.

"Make sure you lock it," he tells me, stepping through the threshold of the door, but then leans in for another quick kiss, as if he's unable to help himself.

After he goes, I rest my back against the door, grinning like an idiot, touching my lower lip with my thumb.

I feel like a fucking schoolgirl with her first crush.

After a quick shower, I jump in bed, listening to the music from the clubhouse until I fall asleep.

Chapter Eleven

"So I've started packing up the house," Ariel tells me, and I can hear Mila making little noises in the background. "Are you sure you are still okay with us moving in?"

"Yes, of course," I assure her. Ariel and Mila are the only family I have left, and I can't wait until they are here.

"Are *you* sure you don't want me to come back and help you?" I ask, not for the first time.

"Yes, you have your own life there, Izzy, don't worry about me. I'm fine. I'm just taking my time and enjoying this stage with Mila, you know? How is everything over there? What's new with the biker gang?" she asks.

"It's not a gang," I grumble, then roll over onto my stomach on the bed, my shoulder holding the phone to my ear. "Yeah, I might have gone there last night for a party."

I hold my breath waiting for her reply.

"You went to the clubhouse?" she asks, not sounding angry or even surprised, maybe just resigned to my current situation. "How was it? What happened? You're clearly alive to tell the tale."

"Yes, I'm very alive," I reply, rolling my eyes. "It was just a really cool party with all the Knights, and a few women were there. Good music, and good food…"

"And good eye candy?"

I picture Renny. "Yeah, definitely good eye candy."

"I can't believe that after living next to them for so long you're finally friends with them. Or is it more than friends with Renny because you're purposely not mentioning him?"

No one knows how to call me out on my shit like my sister.

"I like him," I tell her. "Nothing has happened besides a kiss, but he's cooking me dinner tonight, so we will see how it goes."

"Stay safe, all right? Don't do anything stupid."

"I'm not going to do anything more stupid than I already have," I promise.

I mean, is there anything more stupid than getting drunk and marrying a near stranger?

Oh actually, yes, there is—not telling your big sister about it.

"Good," she sighs. "You know I worry about you."

"And I worry about you, too. Any more run-ins with Mila's sperm donor, or is he back to being MIA?"

"Haven't heard anything from him. It's been peaceful," she admits. "I only hope it stays that way and I'm gone by the time he decides he needs another photo to show his family on his social media."

"It pisses me off that he's probably playing father of the year to them. Meanwhile, he hasn't done a damn thing for Mila," I growl, wishing the man would just disappear from their lives already.

"I know, but he's her father, and that's never going to change. We're going to have to always be the bigger person, for Mila, and to set an example for her. We can't talk badly about him in front of her. That's half of her, whether we like it or not," she says, ever so wise.

"So mature, Ariel, I'm proud of you," I tell her. "But I'm way pettier than you, and she's a baby right now and won't understand what we're saying."

She laughs out loud. "You're right, we can speak freely until she does."

"I miss you," I say, smiling at the sound of her laughter. "I can't wait until you're finally here. We can grow old together."

"What about Renny?" she asks.

"He can live in the garage."

We both laugh at that.

"It's still early times with Renny. I don't know what's going to happen," I admit. "I don't want to have too high expectations because then there's a chance that I'm going to get hurt, but the way he's making me feel right now… I didn't know if I was ever going to meet someone that was going to make me feel that way. You know what I'm usually like with guys—I can take or leave them. It doesn't affect me that much, but the way it's going with Renny… I think he could really hurt me."

"You're such an Aquarius," she mutters. "And I know, he seems different for you, which is why it's so scary. And he's not exactly the man I would have chosen for you. I mean, couldn't you go for a lawyer or a doctor or something? I don't know."

"Easy paths are boring," I respond, laughing. "I didn't choose this, though, Ariel. He fell into my lap. He literally came to the front of my house and into my life. And now that he's here, I don't want to go back to how it was before him."

"I don't think I've ever heard you speak about a man like this," she says, sighing. "You usually just brush it off. I just hope you know what you're doing, Izzy. I'm too old to go around punching your exes in the face; this isn't high school anymore. And Renny is no Larry."

I snicker remembering when my sister punched a boy named Larry in the face after he broke up with me because I wouldn't sleep with him in tenth grade. "I forgot all about that. You're such a good sister, you know that? I don't know what I would have done if I didn't have you looking out for me."

Renny is definitely a whole different ballgame than Larry, but I still don't see Ariel backing down. She's a gentle soul, but when someone she loves gets hurt, she goes into mama bear mode, and nothing or no one can save you from her.

"You looked out for me, too," she says, and I can hear the smile in her voice. "Especially when Mom died."

We go silent for a few moments.

After we say our goodbyes and hang up, I'm about to open my laptop and start my work for the day when there's a knock at the door.

When I open it and see Renny standing there with a bouquet of flowers, I can't wipe the smile off my face.

"Good morning," he says, handing me the beautiful sunflowers. "I'll be here at seven to pick you up, if that works for you?"

"Good morning, and thank you, these are beautiful," I tell him, bringing the flowers to my nose. "And I can just walk over again you know. It's literally down the road."

"We aren't going to the clubhouse," he says with a wolfish grin. "I'm going to take you to my apartment."

"You have an apartment?" I ask, brows furrowing in confusion. "Since when?"

"Since always," he says, putting his hands in his pockets. "I'm hardly there because I'm always at the clubhouse, but when I want a little peace and quiet, that's where I go."

"I was wondering how a romantic evening would work at the clubhouse," I admit. "I was going to tell you that we could come here but you didn't say anything, so neither did I."

"Who said it was going to be romantic?" he asks with a straight face. "I was actually going to make you cook and clean while I played video games."

I roll my eyes. "Try me, I dare you."

He laughs and glances out at his motorcycle, which is sitting pretty on my driveway. "I better get to work, but I just wanted to tell you that I'm looking forward to tonight, and that you look beautiful, and I hope you have a productive day on the couch."

He's standing here in his faded jeans, white T-shirt and boots, and saying everything right. If he doesn't leave soon, I might be having a productive day on the couch, all right.

With him. Under him. All over him.

"Don't look at me like that," he says, brown eyes narrowed to slits. "You're trouble, you know that?"

"Says the outlaw biker," I fire back, distracting myself by smelling the flowers once more. "I can't help it if I find you attractive, and really fucking cute when you do stuff like this. I don't think I've ever gotten 'just because' flowers before, but I've read about them."

Not to mention this is my first time seeing him in something other than black, and it looks good on him.

"You'll be getting them so much now that you'll be sick of them," he promises, leaning forward and giving me a sweet, sensual, yet way too quick kiss. "See you tonight."

"Yes you will," I murmur, staring at his tight ass as he walks away.

I close the door and find a vase for the flowers, suddenly too excited and giddy to concentrate on work.

I need to find something to wear tonight, and it needs to be amazing.

Because tonight is the night I'm going to consummate my marriage.

Chapter Twelve

Crossing the road with my hands full of shopping bags, I enjoy actually being out of the house, wind in my hair and sunshine on my face. After treating myself to a movie and lunch, which is something I know most people don't enjoy doing on their own but something I do for some me time every now and again, I head down the main shopping area in the city, only to be confronted with a hell of a lot of drama.

Pressing myself against the wall of a clothing store, I watch with a crowd as three police officers try to arrest two resisting bikers, a fistfight breaking out in the middle of the street. I eye the bikes and leather cuts and wonder who they are. Even if they were Knights, I wouldn't recognize them, knowing nothing about the patches on their cuts and unable to see their backs to search for the Knights emblem.

A child scurries past me, crying, with no adult around, so I bend down and speak to him. "Are you okay?"

"I can't find my mom," he cries.

"Come here," I tell him, pulling him next to me. "I'll help you find her. Let's just wait until it's safe to walk through." Maybe I can even tell one of the police officers once the men are both safely arrested.

The little boy stops crying, thankfully, probably feeling a little safer now instead of being lost in a crowd. "What's your name?" I ask.

"Billy," he replies, just as I hear the gunshots.

Grabbing him, I pull him in the direction I just came from, away from the crowd and chaos going on in the middle of the street. Everyone is in a panic, women screaming and trying to usher their children out safely. I've never seen anything like this before and my first instinct is to get the hell out of there.

With my back against the wall of a building and Billy crying beside me, I take a deep breath and try to calm myself. I don't know how much time passes, ten, fifteen minutes maybe, but the whole time my mind is running.

Is this normal for bikers? Do they just not care about any kind of authority? Or public safety? What if these men are Renny's friends?

All these questions are running through my head as a blonde woman comes running over to us and pulls Billy into her arms.

"Thank God you're okay. I told you not to wander away from me, Billy. It's not safe." She glances up at me. "Thank you so much."

"No problem," I tell her, forcing a smile. "I think I'm going to go home now, because that's enough drama for one day."

She stands and nods. "The bikers have been arrested and taken away in the police car now, so it's safe. The Destined Killers MC is nothing but no-good criminals. It's not safe to even walk around here anymore." She takes her son and leaves.

Destined Killers MC?

They sound like a lovely bunch.

This is the same brush all bikers are painted with, including the Knights, but it just reminds me that I have no idea who they are. They could have a whole different side to them that I don't know about, and it would be naïve of me to think that they didn't.

"What are you doing, Isabella?" I ask myself as I get into my car.

Deep down I know Renny isn't like that, though. I'd like to think I'm a good judge of character and I haven't picked up on any vibes from him or any of his friends.

He's been nothing but kind to me, and has given me no reason not to trust him.

I need to go with my gut on this one.

And just hope that one day it's not going to be the Knights on the road getting arrested.

"Holy shit," are the first words out of his mouth when he sees me. "I'm not taking you on the bike in that."

I glance down at my short, long-sleeved yellow floral dress and block heels, and frown. I forgot about the whole bike thing. "We can just take my car," I suggest, smiling when I look back up at him and see his eyes still on my legs. It's probably the first time he's seen them bare, besides the time he saw me in a bikini, because I'm usually in jeans.

"Yeah, maybe we should do that," he murmurs, giving me another long once-over. "You look…"

Grabbing my handbag and keys, I try and contain my amusement at his reaction and step outside with him. He offers me his hand, and I take it. I unlock the door, but he opens it for me. "Such a gentleman," I note.

"Not many people would agree with that." He smirks. "You don't mind me driving your car?"

"Not at all," I reply.

He waits until I'm inside before closing the door and heading over to the driver's side. It's weird sitting in your own car with someone else driving, and it's not the best car to start with, and I'm sure he's used to driving much better.

"You need a new car," he says, obviously on the same thought process as me. "This just doesn't seem like something you should be driving."

"It's vintage," I tell him, frowning. "I've had it for years; it's become like a member of the family."

"Well, sometimes family members retire," he says, pulling out of my driveway. "And that doesn't mean we love them any less."

I laugh at that. "You have something to say for everything, don't you?"

"As if you don't," he fires back. "You give as good as you get, and I like that."

"Do you only wear black or white?" I ask, taking in his long-sleeve black sweater and dark jeans.

"No, sometimes I mix things up and wear gray, or navy blue," he replies, eying my bright dress. "Do you ever wear black?"

I nod. "Yeah, my wardrobe has a little bit of everything."

"I like your bright clothes," he admits, shrugging. "It's like a dose of happiness. That's why I got you the sunflowers. They're bright and happy…like you, and pretty much the opposite of me."

"Opposites attract," I say, reaching out and resting my hand on his thigh, a pretty bold move for me. Without missing a beat, he holds my hand, acting like it's something that we do every day. "So what's on the menu to-night?"

"I'm going to make us steak with creamy prawns on top, mashed potatoes, corn and salad," he recites. "And garlic bread."

My eyes widen. "That sounds delicious. And like a lot of food."

"Yeah, so I hope you're hungry."

It's only about a ten-minute drive to his apartment, and I can tell from the outside that it's quite a flashy place by the sheer size of it, and how new the building looks. He parks in his allocated bay and opens the door for me, helping me out of the car. I tug on the hem of my dress as I get out, then walk next to him to the elevator.

"So how many nights a week do you spend here?" I ask him, wondering why he even has his place.

"Maybe once a week? I don't know, it just depends, really," he replies, pressing the button for level ten. "The clubhouse can be filled with so many people at different times, it's just nice to have my own space I can retreat to if need be. Many of the members have their own invest-ment properties and houses, and this is just one I decided to keep for me to use."

Just one of his? Just how much money does the MC have? Now don't get me wrong, I'm no gold digger, and everything I have I've worked my ass off for, but the fact that they are so loaded has me wondering exactly how they make so much money for each member. Or is Renny already independently rich with family money or some-thing like that? Either way, it doesn't bother me, but it does have me curious.

When he opens the door to his apartment and gestures for me to enter, I'm taken aback by how big and lavish the place is. It doesn't look like any other apartment I've been to, with spacious rooms, a stunning white-and-marble kitchen and all light-colored furnishings.

"Did you decorate this place yourself?" I ask him, jaw dropping. "It's beautiful. It looks like a display home."

"No. I hired someone and told them the vision I wanted, though," he admits, pulling a seat out for me at the kitchen table. "Have a seat. Can I get you something to drink? Wine?"

"I'd love a glass of red," I tell him, still taking in my surroundings, in awe of this man's second home. He pours me a glass and sets it in front of me, then starts pulling out ingredients from the fridge.

"Do you want me to help with anything?" I ask, looking toward the hallway, wondering what the rest of the apartment looks like.

"Would you like a tour? You can go have a snoop if you like while I start on dinner," he says, laughing softly.

"Do you mind?"

"Go ahead," he says. "My bedroom is on the right."

"What makes you think that's what I wanted to see?" I call out as I head straight there. I hear him laugh as I open his door and take in the huge four-poster bed. While the rest of the house is light, decorated in white, creams and crystal, his bedroom is the epitome of a man cave, in dark mahogany, leather and furs.

"I hope that fur is fake," I mutter to myself, stepping inside and even having a look in his bathroom, which has the nicest, biggest shower I've ever seen, with two heads and plenty of space for more than one person. If there was an orgy shower, this would be it, which suddenly has me feeling a little suspicious. What if this place is like his sex den, the spot he takes women so he has some privacy and quiet away from the MC?

I suddenly want to set the place on fire.

After checking out the guest room and the laundry, I head back to the kitchen and sit back down. "That's a big shower you have there. How many people can you fit in it?" I ask, eyes slightly narrowed.

Back to me, he laughs. "I don't know, that's never been tested, but it is pretty roomy. I'm guessing you think it's a bit much?"

"No, it's beautiful," I tell him, tone not as enthusiastic as it was when we first arrived.

"But?" he prompts, leaving the stove and moving in front of me. He scans my eyes and then tilts his head to the side. "What's going on in that head of yours?"

"It looks like you designed it for orgies," I blurt out, unable to help myself.

He studies me for a few seconds, and then starts laughing out loud. "Fuckin' hell, Izzy, it was not designed for orgies. I just wanted a big shower. I'm a big man and I like to have some space, and yeah, it's a bit over the top, but why the fuck not?"

"Just saying," I reply, backtracking and feeling stupid now. I clearly have a worry that Renny is some kind of ladies' man, and that he's been with a lot of women, which—even if he has been, I know it's not fair to hold against him, long as he knows how to be loyal when in a relationship. I mean, I've only slept with three men, so my experience might pale in comparison to his, but I still know what I'm doing in the bedroom, so I shouldn't feel nervous. Maybe I'm just trying to self-sabotage, looking for a reason to walk away from this before I get hurt.

"I've never brought a woman here before, Izzy," he

says, leaning over the counter, his face in front of mine, our bodies not touching but our eyes connected. "So if that's what you're worried about, this isn't some secret place I take women for sex. This is my space, and no one has been here besides Saint, who came here looking for me because there was a fuckin' emergency and they needed me."

"I'm sorry," I say, leaning forward and pressing my forehead against his. "I shouldn't assume."

"I'm not an angel, and I've never claimed to be one," he says, pulling back and watching me. "But I'm also not the devil." He grins, flashing me his teeth. "Now I better finish cooking, or you're going to be a very hungry woman."

"Let me help," I say, getting up and moving next to him. "What do you want me to do?"

"You can make the salad, if you like," he suggests, giving me something to do other than overthink. I get the ingredients out and start to make a Greek salad, popping a square of feta cheese in my mouth along the way. Renny puts some music on his phone and the two of us work in the kitchen together.

"We make a pretty good team," he notes as he serves us the plates.

"We do," I agree. "And the food looks amazing."

I only did the salad, the rest was all him, and it's clear he knows what he's doing in the kitchen. I'm impressed.

He's so much more than just a pretty face.

He refills my glass of wine and we dive in. "This steak is amazing."

"It would have been better if you didn't want it burnt."

"Medium to well-done isn't burnt," I say, rolling my eyes. "I haven't had any meat since Vegas."

"How come?"

"I cut down my meat consumption. So I still eat it, just less regularly. Some nights a week I'll have vegetarian meals, too. I like to mix it up a little," I explain.

"You make everything so complicated," he muses, shaking his head at me. "Next time I'll make you my stuffed mushrooms. You'll love those if you're partial to vegetarian dishes."

He's already talking about next time, which makes me smile.

After we finish up, I try to help Renny clean, but he doesn't let me. "I thought you're the messy one, that's what Temper said," I say.

"You remembered that, did you?" he asks, smirking. "I'm trying to be a little better trained, so I cleaned as I went this time. If I don't, the whole kitchen gets trashed, which is probably what he was talking about."

"Hey, if that's the only shit he could find on you, I'd say you're doing quite well," I tease.

"I forgot about the dessert," he murmurs, pulling out ice cream bars from the freezer. We sit down snuggled next to each other on the couch, eating them while something on Netflix plays in the background.

I start to overthink again, wondering if he wants me to stay the night or not, or is he suddenly going to say *okay, it's time to go home*?

I want to stay, or I want him to come back to mine— either or—but how do I know if he wants the same thing?

I hear him make a sound deep in his throat, and look to my left at him, to find him watching me eat my ice cream.

"Do you eat your ice cream like that in public?" he asks, licking his lips. "You're never having dessert at the clubhouse."

"I'm just eating it normally," I say, frowning.

He imitates me, letting his tongue seductively lap at the milky goodness.

"That is not how I look!" I laugh, gently nudging him with my elbow. We end up kind of wrestling and I land over his lap, in the position someone would be in to get spanked, and I can feel that he's hard.

I can also feel that the bulge is *very* large.

I still, not wanting to squirm on his cock any further, and then casually continue to eat my ice cream, which is still safe in my hand.

What a sight we must make right now.

I glance up at him. "You're trying not to spank me right now, aren't you?"

In this position, how can he not? And not to mention I've always been told I have a pretty decent booty.

He nods. "Not sure what the protocol is on that yet."

While laughing, I accidentally spill ice cream all over his T-shirt. "Oops. Sorry." I pause and then add, "I guess you're going to have to remove that now."

He finishes the last bite of his ice-cream bar and then does just that, removing his top and revealing that amazing toned body I got a glimpse of back in Vegas.

"How much do you work out again?"

"We have a gym in the clubhouse, so every other day or so," he admits, shrugging. "I struggle to sleep if I don't tire myself out."

I blink slowly a few times.

I mean, I wouldn't want him to be unable to sleep tonight, so I guess I could take one for the team and tire him out tonight.

I know, it's a hard job, but somebody has to do it.

Sitting up, I move to straddle him and finish the last

bit of my ice-cream bar, then place my hands on each side of his neck.

"So beautiful," he murmurs, before leaning forward and kissing me. He tastes like ice cream and sin, and my hands on his soft skin over his hard body feel like heaven and hell. The kissing soon deepens, and turns heated, and his hands move to the backs of my thighs, sending goose bumps all over my skin as he inches closer and closer to my ass.

Pushing my knees onto the couch, I lift myself up, giving him more access and me more control of the kiss. My breasts pressed against his bare chest, I run my hands through his dark, thick hair, moaning as he sucks on my bottom lip before moving to my neck, trailing his lips down my sensitive skin.

I don't know how it happens, but in a blur of kisses, touching and stroking, I end up naked, pressed back against the couch, Renny on top of me, his hard cock pointing right at me.

"We need to use protection," I tell him, eyes bulging at how big he is. "I'm on the pill, but…"

But I don't know where he has been.

And we might even need some lube, because that is a really fucking huge weapon he has there. He gets off the couch and grabs a condom from somewhere, rips the packet open with his teeth and slides it on like a pro. I think he's going to slide himself inside of me, but he pauses, licking his lips, looking torn.

"I need to taste this pussy first," he says, getting on the carpet—on his knees—and positioning me with my thighs on each side of his head. He starts to lick and suck until I'm wild. I don't think I've ever been this uninhibited before, lifting my hips so he can get more of me, pulling his hair, and all but grinding my pussy against his face. I'm so turned on, so wet and just wanting everything he has to offer and more.

He's made me crazy with lust.

I come louder than I ever have before, whimpering, panting, just blown away by the pleasure this man is giving me. He stands and lifts me in his arms, carrying me back to his bed, to have his wicked way with me. He lays me back and slides inside me, and I'm so dazed and so wet, all I can do is take what he gives me, loving every second of it.

This.

This is what has been missing from my life.

Chapter Thirteen

I wake up feeling deliciously sore, satisfied and hungry. Rolling over, I almost yelp in surprise when I see Renny's face right in front of mine, his eyes still closed.

Shit. It's going to take a little while to get used to sharing a bed with someone, and waking up with them.

Silently stretching, I smile as I think of last night.

We had sex four times.

Four.

I don't think I've ever met a man with such stamina.

That's definitely my new record, but for him, I wouldn't be surprised if he could have kept going. What's more impressive than the four times was the number of orgasms I had.

Five.

That's definitely a record, because it takes me a lot to come, and I usually only come from clitoral stimulation during oral sex, but this guy.

This guy.

He made me come just with his penis.

Either I've been sleeping with guys who are really bad in bed or he's really good, and I'm thinking it might be the latter.

Sitting up, I glance down at him, so boyish in his sleep,

his dark lashes crescents on his face. He's such a good-looking guy, but it's more than that. There's just something about him that makes me feel like I'm in the right place, and I'm feeling pretty lucky this morning.

After sliding out of bed quietly, not wanting to wake him up, I use the bathroom, and have a quick shower and brush my teeth with the toothbrush I was smart enough to pack in my bag when I knew I intended on spending the night with him. He's not in bed when I resurface, back in the same dress from the night before. Instead I find him in the kitchen cooking us breakfast. I enjoy the view for a few moments before letting him know that I'm here, admiring his bare, muscled back and his ass in the gray sweatpants he has on. The tattoos covering him are truly beautiful, even the Knight, which is currently looking right at me.

"Good morning," I say, eyes still on his body. "Is that bacon I smell?"

"Bacon, eggs, hash browns and toast," he says, turning around and opening his arms for me.

Resting my cheek against his chest, I reply with, "Cooking bacon with no shirt on—ballsy, but damn, this is a nice view to wake up to."

"I could say the same," he murmurs, kissing me on the forehead. "Do you want some coffee?"

"Coffee would be amazing. I can make it," I offer, moving toward the kettle.

"Nope, you sit down, I've got this," he says, lifting me up into his arms, carrying me to the barstool and placing me down. "Let a man spoil you a little."

"You're going to be in big trouble if I get used to this," I tease, sitting back and watching him work.

This has been the best first date ever. I tell him as much.

"That's what I was aiming for," he replies, beaming. "Next time, though, I'll take you out somewhere."

"That will be nice. I'll have to cook for you one night this week at my house. I have a few recipes up my sleeve I save for special occasions that I'm quite well known for," I brag.

"I'd love that."

That's two dates we've already set up, and I haven't even left his apartment yet. We have breakfast together, amazing coffee, and then we drive back to my house.

I can't remember the last time I had a date where I left just grinning from ear to ear, and feeling so excited to see that person again.

I must have been doing it wrong this entire time.

"You're glowing today," my mail carrier says as he drops off today's package.

"Why thank you, Frank," I say, smiling. "I'm feeling pretty good today."

Renny drove us home and then walked back to the clubhouse. I made a joke about asking if he needed me to walk him, which I think he found amusing, and after I got changed into some fresh clothes, I've been trying to get some work done. But all I can think about is last night. And Renny. And even the mail carrier can tell that there's something different about me, although I hope he can't tell that it's because I got laid last night.

"Have a good day!"

"Thank you," I say, box in my hands. Closing the door with my hip, I head back to my spot on the couch and am opening my package when my phone rings.

I glance at the caller: Dad.

Yeah, not going to pick that one up.

I don't know why he's calling me, because he usually only calls on my birthday and Christmas, but he's not who I want to talk to right now, because he will definitely put a damper on my good mood. If he wants to ask about Mila, he can call Ariel and ask her himself.

Opening the box, I pull out the new clothes I ordered for Mila—in a bigger size, of course—and place them in the wardrobe of my spare room. Before they get here, I'm going to turn this room into the perfect haven for them both.

Ariel and Mila here.

Renny down the road.

I can't see life getting much better than this.

I wish I could take a photograph of Renny's face every time I offer to pay for something. It's a mixture of confusion, disbelief and offense.

"You haven't let me pay for anything since I met you," I tell him later that day, scowling. "I'm paying for dinner, and that's that. You freaking fixed my car and paid for it. A relationship is give and take. You aren't my sugar daddy, and while I think it's sweet you like to take care of things all of the time, I'm a capable, strong, independent working woman. Even though I might not be loaded and dripping in properties like you, I can afford to take us out to eat."

He opens his mouth to argue, but I flash him a look, one that dares him to press me.

"Izzy—"

I give the waitress, who looks like she'd rather be anywhere else right now, my debit card, while Renny sits there, scowling and silently brooding, what I assume is his version of a man tantrum.

A mantrum.

"I don't like having someone else pay for me," he finally says. "Especially my woman. I'm the man, and I should be paying for our meals or activities. You pay for your own life, your own house and bills and all of that, so let me at least cover anything we do when we're together."

"You paid my mechanics bill," I remind him. "It's 2019, Renny. Modern times. You aren't any less of a man if you let a woman pay for you now and again."

He still looks extremely unhappy, and for a second I wonder if it was worth it, if I should have just let him pay to not spoil what was a beautiful evening up until now, but then I think, no.

Fair is fair.

"Did you think that maybe sometimes I want to spoil you back, too?" I ask, trying a different approach. "I don't want you to put in all the effort—I want to show you how much I like and care about you, too."

"You can do that in other ways," he suggests, a thoughtful expression on his face. "Massages, hugs, cooking…sex."

I roll my eyes. "You're incorrigible, you know that? I paid, you survived it, and that's it. Now stop having a mantrum and ruining the rest of the evening, because we still have to sit through a movie together."

"A what?" he asks, brows pulling together.

"A mantrum. A man tantrum. It's a thing," I say, shrugging.

He starts laughing, softly at first, but then louder. "I seriously never know what's going to come out of your mouth. You know, most people would be too scared to say something like that to me."

"I'm not most people," I reply, arching my brow.

"I know, and I respect that, and you," he says instantly, throwing some money on the table for the tip.

A lot of money.

Which I'm sure is his way of having the last word.

Raising my eyes to his, I state, "I'm paying for the movies."

"No fuckin' chance," is his reply, which he says with a smile. "You paid for dinner, I'll pay for the movies. That's fair, right?"

I eye the money he just dropped on the table for the lucky waitress, which is about the same amount as the entire meal cost in the first place, and shake my head.

"You're a control freak," I decide.

"I'm just old school," he says, shrugging. "That's how my mom raised me, to be a gentleman, open doors…"

"And to pay for shit?" I fill in, smirking. "Well, I'm happy she raised you as a gentleman, and we'll work on the money thing. I guess you're allowed to have one flaw."

"You're the only woman I've met who has considered me wanting to pay for everything a flaw," he grumbles, standing and offering me his hand. "Come on, we better get to this movie."

Taking his hand, I let him lead me out of the restaurant and to his motorcycle. I'm cooking for him tomorrow night, which means three dates in a row.

I've never done anything like that before, but I guess I'm experiencing a lot of firsts since I've met Renny.

Even our first argument over money.

Chapter Fourteen

Knock knock.

Raising my head from my laptop screen, I wonder who could be at the door, unless Renny forgot something when he left this morning.

"Hey," I say when I open the door and see Skylar standing there with food in her hands.

My house hasn't had so much traffic since…well, ever. No one really comes here, but all of a sudden there are people dropping by every day, and surprisingly I don't mind it.

"Hey, are you busy? I picked up some lunch and thought we could hang out," she asks, smiling warmly at me. "Don't be shy to say no and kick me out."

Grinning, I open the door wider. "I'm not busy at all, come on in."

She enters and looks around. "You're really good at decorating," she muses, taking in the bright art on my wall. I've made my space as warm and homey as I can, surrounded by memories and little bits and pieces I've picked up over the years. "Interesting, I wouldn't have pegged you as having a boho style."

"I'm full of surprises."

We sit down at my dining table and she starts to unload the food. "So, I thought we could hang out just us two, because it's hard to get to know someone with all the men around, and it looks like you and Renny are becoming serious. Three date nights in a row? Jeez. Has anything changed now that you guys have actually consummated the marriage?"

"No, nothing has changed," I reply, wincing. "And yeah, I know, apparently we aren't sick of each other just yet."

But that doesn't mean that I want to be married to the man.

"I'm sure it will be fine," she replies, shrugging it off. "Or maybe the two of you will just stay married and live happily ever after and have pretty green-eyed children."

"Yeah, I don't know about all of that." I check the amount of food that she keeps pulling from the bag. "Dude, who else is coming for lunch?"

"I know, but I wasn't sure what you liked, so I thought I'd cover all my bases. Food won't go to waste—I'll just take it back to the clubhouse. Trust me, it will vanish within the second," she says, admiring her spread. "Help yourself. I recommend the burger, personally, but everything is pretty good. It's from the café just down the road from here."

I pick up the burger. "Thank you, this was really nice of you."

"You're welcome, least I can do," she replies, opening the wrapper on her own burger. "Renny says that you're an epic graphic designer. How did you get into that?"

"Just something that I was always good at that I turned into a career," I say, shrugging. "I was always good with editing photos and making little graphics and things like that, and my media teacher actually pushed me toward it when I was in high school. I do enjoy it, and it gives me the freedom to be my own boss. If I didn't have work coming in, though, I'd have to find another real-life job."

Skylar makes a sound of amusement. "A real-life job, hey? I'm a paramedic. I don't think it gets any more real life than that."

"No, you're probably right," I say, grinning. "You must be pretty badass to dive into such a field—you should be proud of yourself."

"I am," she laughs. "I had no idea what I wanted to do for such a long time, but now that I've found it, it's been worth the wait."

We end up chatting for two hours before she stands to leave. "By the way, I asked Renny if he called the lawyers, and he told me to mind my business," she says at the door, scowling. "I told him that I'd call them for you, and he said he will speak to them when he's ready."

"So he hasn't even called them?" I ask, mouth dropping open. "He said he would handle it."

She smirks as she steps through the doorframe. "Guess he likes you being his wife more than he wants to let on."

I grit my teeth but wave bye to her as she heads back to the clubhouse. I don't have many friends that I see regularly, and it was nice to chat with her. While I still speak to several of my high school friends and we usually do monthly catch ups, I don't have a close friend I get to see all of the time. I think Skylar might just become that.

Renny comes over at about seven and I've already started cooking our dinner, so it's too late to cancel. I'm really pissed off that he hasn't even called the lawyers yet. He promised me he would.

"Something smells like it's burning," is the first thing he says to me.

"Fuck," I curse, rushing to the oven to find my chicken now black on top. I was too busy thinking of all the ways I'd tell him off that I burned the fucking thing. "God-dammit."

Renny takes it out of the oven and inspects it. "It will be fine. We'll just cut all the skin off."

"You mean cut all the flavor off," I grumble, sighing. "Man, this was meant to be the best chicken you've ever tasted."

"Izzy," he murmurs, turning my body to face him, hands on my shoulders. "Look at me." I lift my face. "It's just a chicken. There will be other chickens, and it's fine, we can still salvage it. Come on, I'll help you."

Fuck, he can be sweet, but I'm not going to let him get off easily about this lawyer thing. "Did you sort things out with the lawyer yet?"

"I'm waiting for them to get back to me," he replies. "Why?"

Eyes narrowed, I want to call him out on what I heard today, but I don't want to get Skylar into any shit. "Can you give me their number? I'll call them myself, which might hurry it along," I push, seeing what he's going to say next.

"I told you I would handle it, you don't need to worry."

"You did say that, but it's not handled yet, so I'm a little concerned," I fire back, studying him. "I would have thought that you could make things happen a little faster."

I'm pushing him now, but I know he's not being honest about it and he's clearly taking his time, if he's even called them at all.

"Which lawyers are you going through again?"

"Bentley & Channing. The best in the business," he says without a thought.

"And you've called them?" He pauses, and his hesitation is answer enough. "You haven't, have you?"

"It's on my list of things to do," he admits, wincing. "I'm going to get it sorted, I told you that, and I will, okay? Just give me a little time."

"How about you just be honest?" I say, brow furrowing. "Didn't we have this conversation about no games? And here you are lying about calling them. Don't tell me what you think I want to hear, tell me the truth."

"I'm sorry," he says, sighing softly. "But I will take care of it, Izzy. Look, I'll even send them an email right now, asking them to call me tomorrow."

He types out an email on their website contact page, shows it to me, and hits send. "Done."

I'm still not happy about how he's handling this whole thing, but I let it go.

For now, I decide I'll give him the benefit of the doubt.

I don't like the fact that he didn't tell me the truth, though. It's like he thinks he can do whatever he wants and it will be fine, because he isn't actually hurting me, or however he manages to justify it to himself. But life doesn't work like that. He's clearly used to doing what he wants without having to explain himself, but you can't be like that in a relationship. At least not in the type of relationship I want to have.

We save what we can from the chicken and place it on top of the salad. It actually ends up tasting pretty good, even though it wasn't the original meal I had planned. Renny has a proper look around my house and suggests I let him upgrade the security, so he can put in some cameras and a better lock system. I mention to him that I've even been thinking of getting a guard dog, and he tells me he thinks it's a good idea. With my new ties to the MC, I think I need to start being a little more careful.

"I want a do-over of tonight. Don't judge my cooking skills based on this meal, please."

He laughs, shaking his head at me. "Babe, I wouldn't care if you served me two-minute fuckin' noodles, I'll still be here every night if you'll have me."

Our eyes lock and hold.

He pisses me off, makes me question everything and then he goes and says something like that, something that makes it feel worth it.

Only time will tell if that's true or not.

The next time I invite him over for dinner, I make sure that I've pre-cooked everything beforehand so there is room for error in case anything goes wrong this time around. It doesn't, and my lasagna turns out perfect. Renny shows up with dessert, flowers and a sexy smile.

"How was your day?" I ask him, rising on my toes to give him a kiss. I haven't seen him since last night, and although I'd hate to admit it, I spent a lot of today thinking about him.

"Good. We sold a few more bikes," he says, handing me the beautiful mixed bouquet of flowers. "And these are for you."

"Thank you," I say, smelling the flowers and then eying the cheesecake in his hands. "You bring me the best gifts, they're beautiful. What's the occasion?"

He grins and glances down at the dessert. "Just because. How about your day? Did you actually get any work done, or did you procrastinate?"

"I got some work done," I admit, wincing. "But I also

cleaned out my entire linen cupboard and organized it all into labeled categories."

He laughs softly and follows me into the kitchen. "Nothing smells like it's burning."

"Very funny," I say, organizing the flowers into a vase and turning to face him. "Are you hungry now?"

"Always," he replies, glancing down my body.

"Food first." I smirk and settle the lasagna, garlic bread and salad on the table, hoping he loves my mom's recipe.

"Smells good. Can I help with anything?"

"Nope, just take a seat," I reply, grabbing two plates and cutlery and joining him at the table.

"I missed you today," he says, staring at me over the food. "You should come and work in the shop office, and then I can sneak in and annoy you and bring you food."

I roll my eyes but secretly think he's pretty damn cute right now. "That's a little codependent, don't you think?"

"You're the most independent woman I know, I don't think you could be codependent with anyone," he replies, lip twitching.

"I don't know, I'm getting pretty needy with Mila," I tease, serving him a big slice. "I want to cuddle her at least ten times a day. And, Renny?"

"Yeah?"

"I missed you, too," I admit, looking him in the eye.

I don't know how the hell this happened, but I think I'm falling for this man.

Shit.

"Happy birthday, dear Temper, happy birthday to you," the crowd sings to the birthday boy's displeasure. He didn't want a party or a cake, but he got both anyway, and everyone seems to delight in spoiling the man who would probably rather be alone to celebrate. I can't help but smile, seeing him sit in front of a cake covered in thirty-five candles, and someone even put a fucking party hat on him.

"Hip hip, hooray! Hip hip, hooray!" everyone cheers, clapping as he blows out each and every candle. Skylar passes him a knife and he cuts the first slice before she takes over and cuts the rest of the cake up for everyone to eat.

"Thank you all for coming," Temper calls out, cracking a smile. "I couldn't be surrounded by a better bunch of people."

"This cake is amazing," I tell Renny, licking my lips.

He groans next to me. "You're seriously the most sensual eater I've ever seen. And I don't think I've ever seen anyone enjoy food as much as you do."

I purposely lick some vanilla frosting off my fingers. "Let me eat my cake in piece, Renny."

He makes a choking sound deep in his throat. "I'm going to get a drink. Do you want something?"

"Bottle of water, please," I tell him.

After finishing the cake, I head to the bathroom to wash my sticky fingers. I stop in my tracks when I hear my name. I can hear Renny's and Dee's voices as they stand on the other side of Renny's bedroom door, the door I was about to walk into.

"What the hell are you doing, Renny?" Dee says. "You weren't meant to fall for her."

"You think I don't know that?" Renny replies, sounding extremely unhappy going by his dire tone. "But she's mine, and that's the end of it. Messing with her car that day was the best thing I've ever done."

"Now isn't the time to talk about this."

Messing with my car? Are you kidding me right now? He's the reason it wouldn't start? What if something happened to me? Did he not care if he put me in danger?

Anger, betrayal and hurt hit me, right in the chest, the impact causing me to lean against the wall for support. This relationship with him felt too good to be true, and I guess it was, but I still don't understand what they had to gain from this.

It makes no sense.

What does Dee mean, Renny wasn't meant to fall for me?

Renny exits the room and sees me standing there. "What is he talking about?" I ask him.

Dee comes up behind him, wincing when his eyes land on me. "Fuck, Izzy—"

"Tell me," I demand.

Renny reaches out to touch me, but I step back. He hasn't been honest about something, and I need to know what it is, I need to know if everything between us is real. If he wasn't meant to fall for me, what was he supposed to do with me? Is it not a coincidence that I am here right now?

What use could I be?

Dee quickly makes an exit, leaving me alone with the man I only just thought I was falling in love with. How things can change in an instant. I went from inexplicably trusting him to not being able to look him in the eyes without it hurting.

"You tampered with my car?" I ask, gritting my teeth. I mean, who does that?

"I did," he admits, eyes filled with pain. I'm sure that they mirror my own right now, brown at war with green.

"I wanted you to trust me, and I wanted an excuse to talk to you."

"Why?" I ask, tone harsh even to my own ears. "You could have just said hello, like a fucking normal person. Why did you fuck with my car, Renny? You could have put me in danger! Did you even think of that? Or were you too busy just thinking about your damn club?"

He exhales before answering me. "You weren't in danger. I just crimped the fuel line, and you had no gas in there, so the car wasn't going to move. I'm surprised it even made it out of the driveway. We came up with a plan that we would make friends with you, get you to trust us and then… I don't know, okay? We didn't even know what we were going to do, but we know who your dad is, and we know that's going to be useful to us. He's a powerful man. With the shit going on with our MC right now, if we had him at our backs it would benefit us."

My dad. Of course.

I didn't even think of that, because I rarely connect myself to him.

I thought Renny was my Knight in shining armor. Instead he's just a lying biker in leather.

"Well, unfortunately for you, I have nothing to do with my father, and he couldn't care less if anything happened to me, just in case your mind was wandering toward kidnapping me for ransom or some shit like that," I fire at him, stepping closer to him and lifting my head so I'm looking him right in the eye. "I never want to speak to you again. You are dead to me."

And that's how a Knight broke my heart.

Chapter Fifteen

There's a reason I don't tell anyone my dad is the mayor of the city I live in. We have different surnames, because I took my mom's maiden name, so no one normally figures out the tie between us. But the MC obviously got their hands on that information somehow.

Ariel and I cut off ties with him long before the cancer took my mom. We stopped talking to him when he left her for his mistress after years of affairs, treating her less than she deserved. He's not a good man. I do think he loves us, in his own way, but it's not enough. He's known for being a dirty mayor, and yes, for being powerful with his connections, too. I can see how having an in with him would benefit the MC, because he does control a lot of what happens in this city, and having him on their side would be an asset.

I've never felt so used, though, and so betrayed. I thought Renny was…well, the one. My one. I'd never been so hopeful in love than I was less than twenty minutes ago, and now I'm sitting on my couch, crying, alone and destroyed.

I know he followed me home to make sure I got there safely after I ran out of the clubhouse, but I don't care. I know he's hurt, too, but it's too bad, because he caused this.

"What did I do to deserve this?" I whisper to myself, taking a deep breath. I'm a good, honest person. I don't lie, I don't cheat.

They went as far as to break my car so they could fix it and I would feel indebted to them. That's going above and beyond in the betrayal department. That's manipulative, cunning and well planned. Did they sit at a fucking drawing board, trying to make a plan on how to make me fall in love with Renny so they could use me however they saw fit? Did they even need to go to Vegas, or was that all bullshit, too? Were they going to use me to blackmail my father? I have no idea, and neither did they, I think.

Their plan was simple: Use Isabella.

And Renny was the one they sent to execute it.

And how well he did.

Even though it's late, I pick up the phone and call Ariel. Along with Renny, I just lost everyone I've been spending my time with and giving my energy to, including Skylar. The whole thing hurts, and to be honest right now, I just want to leave.

Maybe I should.

After speaking to Ariel, I do the one thing I never thought I'd do: I book a flight.

That's how badly I need to get out of here. I'm going to face my biggest fear—flying—because the thought of that is less scary and painful than the thought of Renny.

Rather than deal with the fallout of what's happened with the MC, I'm going to run.

Tag, you're it.

"Mila, you're the best thing in my life right now," I tell her, blowing raspberries on her little stomach. "I missed you, beautiful girl."

"You know you're going to have to face him eventually," Ariel says to me, standing in the doorframe, watching me play with her daughter. "He's your neighbor. This is why they say don't shit where you live."

"I didn't shit. He did," I reply, sitting up and turning to her. "I know, Ariel. I just need a little time to get over him so I'm not weak and can just pretend I don't know him."

"Very mature strategy," she replies, rolling her eyes.

"Maybe I should sell my house and move away. We could live by the beach or something. Far away from betrayal on a motorcycle."

"Dad always told us to be careful with who we trusted," she sighs, coming to sit down on the other side of the bed. "I'm sorry this happened, Izzy. It's not going to be easy for you, but you're going to be okay. You're a good person, and you're beautiful inside and out. You deserve someone who wants nothing from you but your love."

"I know," I agree. "I just have to wonder if it was all fake, because if it was, then he deserves a fucking Oscar for the performance he gave me."

She's quiet for a few moments before she replies. "I don't think it was. I do think he cares about you, but he didn't come into this for that. I think it just happened. I think he obviously thought you were attractive, but like you overheard, he started falling for you, which wasn't the plan. But in the end that obviously won out over anything else."

"That doesn't justify it."

"No, it does not," she agrees, nodding thoughtfully. "He had an ulterior motive, clearly, but did he ever ask you about Dad? Or for anything?"

"No," I admit, glancing down at Mila, who is sucking on her fingers. "He never asked anything about Dad, which I don't get. Shouldn't he have been trying to get information on him from the get-go? This whole thing just makes me feel so yucky, you know? I would have done anything for that man."

And I guess that was the point.

If the club got into shit and they needed Dad's help, I probably would have reached out to him and asked for it, because I would have wanted to help and support them in any way I could.

And that's exactly what they wanted.

Renny didn't even have to ask about Dad—it would have been me thinking of that plan, so I would have thought it was my idea, not theirs.

I mean, I can't guarantee what would have happened and if Dad would have helped, or what the fallout would be if he knew I was dating a biker. But for them, for Renny, I would have tried.

And I would have been an idiot, because that's the only reason they wanted me around, to use as a wild card, to try to save them if they ever needed it.

Their secret backup plan.

"We don't know what he's thinking because you never let him explain," Ariel points out, eyes gentle on me. "Don't get me wrong, nothing excuses him for what he's done, but I don't know… Have you checked your phone since you left? I'm sure he's trying to contact you so he can try to explain what happened from the start."

"No, I haven't," I grumble, crossing my arms over my chest. "And I don't want to. I don't care if he's trying to contact me. I don't owe him anything, even an explanation on my whereabouts."

"He did one good thing for you," she adds, grinning.

"What?"

"He made you get on your first flight in fifteen years."
She laughs, shaking her head at me. "Let me tell you, I
thought that day would never come, but it did and you
survived it."

"Barely."

I didn't tell her I had a few alcoholic beverages in the
airport before I boarded the flight, but I did, and they did
help. Still, I was terrified, and now have marks on my
palms from where my nails dug into them. I was scared,
but I wanted to be away from home so badly, and I knew I
had to stick it out to do that. I could have driven, but that
car is tainted for me now, and God knows what they did
to it. Besides, let him see my car there and wonder where
I am. Let him hurt as much as he has hurt me.

All is fair in love and war.

"Are you going to fly home?" she asks, picking up
Mila and gently tapping her on her back. "I guess you
could take a bus."

"I haven't thought that far ahead," I admit. I know
I'm going to have to go back and be an adult, and I can't
just have my house sitting there alone and unattended,
but right now I'm just enjoying the distance. Even if it is
an avoidance technique, I'm going to use it for now. "At
least this time I brought my laptop so I can work, and I
can help you pack up the house so you don't have to do
it alone. Or I can watch Mila while you pack, because I
know how long that takes you."

"You know I'm happy to have you back here," she
says, smiling at me. "But you look so sad, and I want to
fix it for you, but I can't. I was hoping he'd look after
you, which he did in some ways but apparently not in
others. I don't know. Can I call him up and yell at him?"

Laughing, I tell her no. "Besides, I'm going to ghost his ass. That means no contact, and basically I'm going to act like he never existed."

Ariel grabs my phone from her side table and puts in my code.

"How do you know my code?"

"You use the same code for everything," she replies, rolling her eyes. "And you have since high school."

It's true. Dammit.

"He has called you fifteen times, and you also have missed calls from Skylar," she says, scrolling through. "And ten messages in your inbox."

Sighing, my shoulders drooping, I wonder if I've made the right move, or if I should just hear what he has to say. If I don't, this is just going to drag on and on, and if I'm going to get over him and move forward, I'm going to need some closure on the whole thing.

"Are you going to put him out of his misery?" she asks, watching me. "Or are you going to continue to make him suffer?"

"I'll hear him out," I decide. "But only so that we can just move on and forget this whole fake relationship ever happened."

I'll sort out the annulment myself, since he seems to be taking his sweet time with it, probably so he can tell Dad he's married to me now. He's probably telling everyone that the mayor is his father-in-law.

"Izzy," Ariel chastises, frowning at the phone. "He's calling, so now's your chance."

She hands me the phone, and with a deep gulp I press accept. "Hello?"

"Izzy, where are you? Your car is here, but you're not home," he says, sounding worried.

"How do you know I'm not home? Did you break in and check?" I ask him, pursing my lips.

When he goes silent, I know that he did exactly that. "You are unbelievable, you know that? You think no rules apply to you and that you can do whatever the fuck you want with no repercussions!"

"I just wanted to see if you were okay, and try to speak to you about what happened—"

"You mean me finding out the truth that you broke my car, lied to me over and over again, and planned on using me to get to my dad and his connections?" I ask, cutting him off. "I never thought you were anything but genuine, Renny. Perhaps you should become an actor?"

"That's not fair," he says, sounding angry now. "Yes, I went into this with different intentions, but when I met you, everything changed. The conversation you heard was nothing new to me—the men have been giving me shit about this the entire time because I told them I had feelings for you. I also told them that no one was to go near you or say anything to you, and that if we wanted to save Temper's brother, then we will have to find another way."

Temper's brother? What does he have to do with any of this? I make a mental note to ask about this after I get to the bottom of my part in it.

"So everyone knows? And I'm some laughingstock to the MC? They all sat with me, laughed with me, got to know me, and they all knew I was only there because everyone wanted to see what you can get out of me?" I ask, yelling now.

He goes silent. "Temper didn't know and Skylar didn't know, but yes, the rest of the men knew."

Temper didn't know? So they all did this without the approval of their president?

"Well, you're all a bunch of assholes," I say, my tone going flat. "You know, if this whole thing had been genuine, and my car really had just broken down, and everything was true, I would have done anything to help you and the MC. I can't believe you would use people like that. It's so unattractive, and not the person I thought you were."

I know he said that he told the men the plan wasn't going to go ahead and that I was his, as I overheard, but it doesn't change how we came about.

It doesn't change anything.

He still tampered with my car, still acted like it was a coincidental meeting, like it was fate playing its hand when really it was a really well thought out, elaborate plan to get me under his thumb… How am I meant to forgive that?

Chapter Sixteen

"I'm sorry," he whispers, taking a deep breath. "I am so fucking sorry that this is how we met, but I'm not sorry I met you. Everyone at the MC knew that I thought you were so fuckin' beautiful, which is why when Dee came up with the idea I wasn't going to let any of the other men come near you—"

"How considerate of you," I snarl, shaking my head. "You didn't know me then, and that you couldn't have known we would end up having such a connection, but the fact that you would do that to someone, anyone…that doesn't sit well with me, Renny. I don't know what you want me to say, or do, or how I'm meant to get over this. How can you expect me to? I've been nothing but honest and myself with you, and to find out that I didn't get that back in return? It's heartbreaking."

"I know," he says, sounding hurt. "Trust me, I know. But I'm fuckin' crazy about you. I know I can't expect you to get over this, but you can't expect me to just let this go either. I've never felt about anyone the way I do about you, and I'll do anything to make this up to you."

"I don't know if there is a way to make this better," I say, swallowing hard. "I'm safe, you don't need to worry about me, and I'll be home when I'm ready."

"Izzy—"

"Goodbye."

I hang up before he can say anything else, then glance up at Ariel, who was listening to the entire conversation.

"Come here," she says, placing Mila down in her crib and opening her arms for me. "It's all right."

She rubs my back while I cry. I've never felt so weak, and I hate that he did this to me.

How dare he?

I was right, he was trouble from the beginning, and I should have trusted my gut instinct and stayed away from him. I should have resisted temptation, but I didn't, and now I have to pay the price.

God help the next man who tries to love me.

"Dad is calling me again," Ariel says, frowning. It's been a week since I spoke to Renny. A very long week. "What do you think he wants?"

"I don't know, he called me last week, too," I admit, shrugging. "Maybe he's having another kid or something."

After my dad married his mistress, Angie, and moved in with her and her children, he went on to have two more kids with her, another two little girls. I've only seen my half sisters a handful of times over the years and am not really close to them, which is sad because they did nothing wrong. My dad's brother once joked that my dad must have done something terrible in a past life to be given four daughters and no sons, which kind of shows what type of men they are.

On top of all the bad blood with our father, Angie hates us and will go out of her way to make us feel like we don't belong anywhere near their family. When Mom was alive Angie was rude and nasty to her, and tried to rub in her face that she stole her husband.

"A good man can't be stolen," my mom replied to her once, and that line has always stuck with me, because it's true. A good man can't.

"How many kids does he need?" Ariel grumbles, then sighs and picks up. "Hello? Hey, Dad. Yeah, I know, I've been really busy." She pauses. "Ummm, no, why? What have you heard about Isabella?"

Oh, fuck.

"Nope, I don't know anything about bikers, Dad, but you know she lives near them, so maybe that's why someone is saying that," she lies, looking at me with wide eyes. "Of course I'm looking after her, someone has to."

And there it is.

None of our conversations can end civilly. The past is always brought up, the bad blood between us seeping through.

"Yes, I will make sure Isabella is making good decisions and not riding on the back of criminal bikers' motorcycles so it doesn't look bad on you. Anything else, Dad?" More pausing. "Okay then, until next time. By the way, your first granddaughter is doing well, thank you for asking."

She hangs up, her jaw tense. "He is such an asshole. How did we come from his sperm?"

"I have no idea," I admit, pursing my lips. "At least he gave us nice green eyes and thick dark hair."

She laughs, relaxing a little. "Someone apparently saw you on the back of Renny's bike and told him, that's why he's been calling. He said for us not to do anything that will make him look bad."

"Yeah, because his cheating looked good for him?" I

groan, scowling. "He's a piece of work, isn't he? If only the MC knew the truth. They would probably have better luck on their own making some shady deal than using me to get to him."

Sad, but so true. It's been years since I even felt like I had a father, which is hard when I see him all over the media and on billboards around the city. I kind of learned to bury it and to disassociate myself with him and his life, which is maybe why this whole thing is such a kick to the chest. I can't believe someone saw me and reported back to him, especially when we have nothing to do with him.

"I wonder what they need him for," Ariel muses.

"Renny said something about Temper's brother needing some help, but he also said Temper didn't know about their plan for me. Maybe they were trying to help him, I don't know," I reply, my mind racing. I've never heard of Temper's brother being mentioned before, but they obviously all don't speak freely in front of me. "Dad has a lot of connections."

"Must be important for them if they went through this whole thing just to try to help him," she replies, shrugging. "And knowing Dad's influence, he probably could help them."

My lips tighten. "Are you saying I should help them? You heard Dad just now—he doesn't want me being associated with them. What makes you think he's going to help them for me? He hasn't done anything for me except show me the type of man I never want to marry."

"I'm not saying you should do anything," she replies, studying me. "I'm just thinking out loud here. I know you, if you can help, you're probably going to help."

I puff out a breath. "I like Temper, and he didn't know about what was going on, so he and Skylar are the only

Knights who aren't on my shit list right now. But I just don't see how I can help, Ariel. And I don't see *why* I should. For all we know Temper's brother could be a murderer or something."

"Yeah, maybe," she murmurs, glancing down at her phone. "I don't know how you got yourself into this mess, but now we're going to have to get out of it. Renny is going to fight for you, Izzy, like he said, but eventually he will give up, and you need to make sure that you're truly going to be okay with that."

"I'm perfectly fine with that," I tell her, scowling as I think of him. "He played me, and I'm not going to give him a chance to do that a second time. I'd never be able to trust him and I'd always be wondering if he has ulterior motives..."

I'll miss him, that's for sure, but I'm just going to have to deal with it, because that's not a reason to forgive someone if they don't deserve to be forgiven.

I spend the next few days helping pack and clean up the house, or looking after Mila while Ariel does so. My sister agrees to move back with me sooner than she planned, which means once I head back home I will have her with me. That makes me feel much better about life.

I'm singing softly to Mila when there's a knock at the door. "Ariel! Can you get that?"

"Yeah," she calls back and jogs to the door with packing tape in her hand. "What are you doing here?" I hear her say, and my hackles instantly rise.

"Who is it?" I call, frowning.

"Merve," she replies, sounding extremely unimpressed.

I glance down at Mila, her big green eyes staring up at me, and sigh. "You're in for a world of pain, my love, just like Ariel and me."

The cycle we promised would never continue has, and now Mila has a similar unstable, in-and-out-of-her-life father like we have. But where our dad has ambition, Merve just has stupidity, which he proves as he pushes into the house, eyes coming to me and Mila.

"I just want to see my daughter," he says, clearly unhappy that I'm still here. "Not that I have to explain myself to you."

"You can't just show up here whenever you feel like it, Merve," Ariel tells him, coming to stand next to me. "If you want to see her, message and organize it properly."

"I don't have to do that," he says with a shrug. "It's not like you're doing anything anyway. Are you so busy that I have to schedule in a date with my own fucking child?"

"Do you only have a daughter when it suits you?" I ask, narrowing my eyes. "Need more social media likes? What are you really doing here, Merve, because I think we all know you don't really care about Mila. So cut the shit."

He lifts his chin and crosses his arms. "Does it matter? She's *my* daughter, Izzy, and you guys can't keep her from me even if you wanted to."

"No one is keeping you from her," Ariel tells him, moving closer to me and Mila. "I'm just saying that this is my house and you can't show up every few weeks whenever you feel like it. It doesn't work that way."

He comes closer to us, and I can smell the alcohol on him from here.

"Are you drunk? Because there is no way you're coming near my niece if you are." I quickly hand Mila to Ariel and stand in front of them. "I'm going to call the police if you don't leave—now. Come back when you're sober and then you can hold her."

Hopefully we'll have moved away by then, because he doesn't even deserve to breathe the same air as Mila.

I slide my phone out of my pocket and hit the keypad. "What's it going to be? Do you really want to be arrested right now? I'm sure our dad could make sure you're put away for longer if he feels like it."

Great, now I'm using the Dad card.

How the mighty have fallen.

The threat must work, though, because he swears at us but then leaves. We lock the door behind him, but share a look with each other. Something has to give. "You can't keep going on like this," I say.

"I know," she replies. "I need to get sole custody of her, and I need it now."

I nod. She's right.

We're going to have to do what we need to do to keep her safe.

Chapter Seventeen

Three Weeks Later

"I didn't get to finish your room," I tell Ariel, opening the door and showing her the progress that I had made. "I figure that you can put the crib in the corner, and I'd already started stocking the cupboard with clothes for Mila."

"You're so cute, you know that?" She beams, sitting down on the queen-sized bed. "It feels good to be here, a fresh start, you know?"

It may be a fresh start for her, but for me, I'm going to have to face Renny, and everything that I left behind. After that one conversation I never spoke to him again, ignoring all of his messages and calls. I haven't even read any of the messages, and although it did take a lot of willpower, I just didn't want him to sweet talk his way out of what he did, because there are no excuses for it.

"Someone You Loved" by Lewis Capaldi plays as we unpack Ariel's belongings and it doesn't help the situation one bit, my mind unable to escape Renny knowing that he's just down the road again and that we have unfinished business between us. Part of me wants to hide, and the other part of me wants to storm into that clubhouse and give everyone who looked me in the eye and lied a piece of my mind. If I hadn't overhead that conversation with Dee and Renny, I might have never known the truth, and I would have looked like an idiot to the club for the rest of my life. One of my biggest fears in a relationship is someone making a fool out of me, and Renny did just that.

We've only been home for a few hours when he shows up, knocking unapologetically at my door. He must have seen Ariel's car here and knew I was back.

I open the door, and there he stands, dressed in all black, a scowl on those lips I once loved kissing, brown eyes staring daggers at me. "Yes?" I ask him, my tone saccharine sweet.

"Seriously?" he asks, giving me a quick once-over. "That's all you have to say right now? Yes?"

"It's more polite than what I really want to say," I reply, shrugging. "I'm helping my sister unpack, so if you don't mind, I'd like to have this confrontational conversation another time. Maybe next month? I'll have to check my schedule."

Without missing a beat, he pulls me against him, and kisses me. I push at his chest, but my lips move against his, giving him mixed signals. I don't know what to think or feel right now. I'm angry, I'm hurt, and I've missed him, which only pisses me off even further. Things are so complicated, and I don't know if I should follow my heart or my head.

Eventually, sanity reaches me and I push him off. "What do you think you're doing?"

"I missed you," he says, scanning my eyes. "Like really fuckin' missed you. Let me take you for a ride so we can speak."

"I just said I'm busy," I tell him, frowning. "Look, we obviously do need to speak, but not right now. I want to get Ariel and Mila settled in first—they literally just got here."

"Do you need any help? I hope you two aren't carrying heavy shit," he says, brows drawing together. "Tell me what you need."

"I don't need anything, we have it all under control," I assure him, pursing my lips. "Don't worry about me, Renny. We can talk later."

"How am I meant to not worry about you? You left before we could speak, without telling anyone you were leaving or where you were going, so we didn't even know if you were safe or not. Of course I'm worried about you, about us, about fuckin' everything, and I want to make sure that you're okay," he says, shifting on his feet. "Fuck, Izzy, you sure know how to make someone feel bad."

"And you sure know how to lie and use people," I fire back, eyes narrowing. "Don't try to blame any of this on me, Renny. You fucked up, you lied, and you made me think you were a fucking hero when you've been the villain all along."

"I prefer anti-hero," he grumbles.

"Villain," I repeat, smirking. "You're a wolf in sheep's clothing."

He taps his hands on his chest, on his leather. "I'm a biker—how the hell did you ever think I was a sheep? I'm a Knight, Izzy, and I know you've heard about us."

"Fine, that was a bad analogy," I say, waving my hand into the air. "I just thought at the end of the day you were a good man and that I could trust you, and now you've broken that trust. There's no coming back from that."

His lips tighten. "I'll come and pick you up tomorrow at lunchtime."

"I'm busy tomorrow. How about next week?"

"Izzy—"

"What? I owe you nothing, Renny. And don't look at me like I do," I snap, lips pursing.

"You don't owe me anything, and I never said you did. I just want a chance to speak to you, and that's all," he says, taking a deep breath as if to calm himself.

"I need some time before we have this conversation, okay?" I need to wait until it doesn't hurt when I look into his eyes, but I think that's probably going to take longer than he's going to give me.

"Okay," he says, ducking his head. "Next week then."

"Can't wait," I reply sarcastically, watching him walk away and back down the road toward the clubhouse. I don't know what he thinks we have left to discuss, because I don't think that we're going to get past this.

Some things you just can't take back.

He does and doesn't give me a week.

Although he doesn't come and see me directly, every day he sends something to the house.

Day One: sunflowers.

Day Two: red roses.

I appreciated Day Three, a bottle of expensive vodka and a food hamper filled with bagels, doughnuts and other baked goods.

Day Four was special, though. Instead of getting something for me, he sent presents for Ariel and Mila. And not just normal presents—he sent her a voucher for a chef to come in and cook for a month, and a voucher for a cleaner to come in and clean our house for a month, too.

I don't think I've seen Ariel so happy. Mila was spoiled with a gift certificate for the biggest toy shop in our city.

Day Five was back to me, and a low blow with a marble-framed photograph of us, a photo taken on our wedding night. Even drunk, we both look good, and like a happy couple.

Day Six I got a brand-new laptop, one that is perfect to do my graphic design work on, and which I've been eying for the last few months but couldn't afford. Damn him.

Day Seven I don't know what to expect, but when he arrives on my doorstep with an envelope in his hands, I wonder what he's up to now.

"You need to stop wasting your money, I don't need your gifts," I say, crossing my arms.

"I think this one you will really want," he says, expression blank as he hands me the envelope.

Hesitating, I take it from him and rip it open, pulling out the document and reading it.

"You finally did it," I say, reading the approved annulment papers. After I sign these, we are officially no longer married. Lowering the piece of paper, I look him in the eye. "Thank you, Renny."

It's a bittersweet moment.

This is something I have wanted and pressed for from the beginning, but I can't deny the little bit of sadness that I feel right now. Either way, it was the right thing to do, regardless of where our relationship goes. If I'm going to get married, I want to do it right, not when I'm drunk and barely remember it.

"You're welcome. And I know it doesn't fix things, and I know you're still mad at me and you have every right to be. I just wanted to show you that you can trust me." He takes my hand and looks me in the eye. I see remorse and a little bit of trepidation. "Please, will you let me explain things to you? Just hear me out."

Shifting on my feet, I sigh. I know it's time for me to hear what he has to say. I've put it off long enough. "Okay, how about tomorrow? I have some work due tonight that I need to finish."

He nods. "Great. Tomorrow."

I watch him walk away, then glance back down at the annulment papers.

Why does everything have to be so complicated?

Nerves hit me when I hear his motorcycle.

"I'll be back soon," I tell Ariel, who is nursing Mila. "Wish me luck."

"Good luck," she calls out. "Hopefully you don't kill him. Is he coming in here? Because I might throw my shoe at him if he does. It would have been more than a shoe, but that was before he sent me presents."

"You are so easily bought. Well, on that note, I'll meet him outside," I say, exiting and closing the door behind me. He's taking his helmet off when I approach, and eyes my boyfriend jeans, black belt and thin red knit sweater. He grins and hands me my helmet.

"Where are we going?" I ask.

"For a little ride," he replies. "I'll take us somewhere quiet to talk."

"Okay." Probably good so that no one can hear me yell. "Let's do this."

Being pressed up against him on the bike brings back fond memories, and I make sure not to lean into him like I used to. I don't want him to think that everything is fine and that I'm over what happened, because I'm not.

I'm sure I'll forgive him eventually, but I'll never forget, and it will probably always be something between us.

After about fifteen minutes Renny stops at a big park, with beautiful gardens and a lake. It's the type of place someone might get married at, and I wonder what made him choose it as our place to talk. We're both silent as we get off his bike and walk side by side down the path. He leads the way to a large, beautiful tree, and we sit under it.

"I never meant to hurt you," he starts, studying my profile while I stare out at the ducks on the lake. "I know it was a shitty thing to do to anyone, but once I met you, I knew I would never do anything to hurt you, Izzy. I know I've fucked up and broken your trust, and I'm sorry. But please know I told them straight away that we weren't going through with the plan, because I wasn't going to do that to you. It didn't feel right."

"And what was the plan?" I ask, turning my head so I can look him in the eye. "You never said what the exact plan was, and knowing the MC, there had to have been one. Was marrying me part of it? To get me drunk and then tie the knot to get to my dad, so you'd be married to his daughter and could use that against him?"

"No!" he exclaims, looking surprised. "Us getting married was not part of any plan, and I'm pretty sure it was your idea. How could you think that?"

"How could I not?" I ask. "It works to your advantage, does it not? You could have called him up and told him you were going to make it public that his daughter married an outlaw biker. He probably would have given you anything you wanted to keep that quiet."

He takes a deep breath. "After I met you, everything changed. Nothing else mattered. What we had planned no longer mattered. I wish you could see that. I had the club on my back to try to use your dad's connections to help save Temper's brother, but I couldn't do that to you. I couldn't use you. And I wouldn't. So yeah, I went into this with ill intentions, but I never went through with any of it, and I've given you all of me from the moment you got on my bike. I didn't hurt you, Izzy. I couldn't."

"Where is Temper's brother?" I ask.

"He's in jail," he admits, sighing. "He didn't do what he has been accused of, and now his kids have been put in foster care, and the whole thing is a cluster fuck. But that's not your problem, it's ours, and we'll handle it within the club."

Temper's nieces and/or nephews are in foster care but he doesn't want me to worry about that? I've just become an aunt, and it's one of the most important roles of my life. They've made this my problem and I can't just pretend I don't know about it.

"What is he accused of doing?"

"Someone planted drugs in Trade's house," Renny explains. "And before you ask how I know he's not guilty, Temper's mom died of an overdose in front of both of them. Neither have ever touched any drugs. So trust me when I say Trade is not fucking around with having drugs in his house with his kids."

"Who would want to frame him?" I ask, curious.

"We don't know. Could be another MC, the cops… We aren't sure. Someone was out to get him. It could even be his ex-wife, who lost custody of the kids and wasn't happy about it. Trade used to be heavily involved with the Knights, but when he became a full-time dad he left the lifestyle behind," he says. "He's still a Knight, and always will be one, but he stepped away, and we all respected that."

Shit. "How am I supposed to believe everything you're saying right now?" I ask, lifting my chin.

He cups my cheek and looks me in the eye. "You know me, Izzy, and some part of you still trusts me. Otherwise you wouldn't be here right now, sitting alone in the middle of nowhere with me. If you truly thought I was capable of holding you as a ransom or kidnapping you, would you be next to me right now? You heard what I was saying to Dee, but you also heard him saying that I'm falling for you, and that I've gotten myself into a shitty spot because of my feelings for you. So you know that what's between us is real, and you can't deny that."

He makes some valid points, but I don't know, it feels like before we were a fairy tale and now we're just your average fucked-up couple. Okay, maybe not average, but you know what I mean.

"I'm not denying anything," I say, swallowing hard. "I was falling for you, too, and I think you knew that. But now I don't know what I'm supposed to do. I just need some time to think. I don't know if I can trust you again, and without trust, we have nothing."

"You can have all the time in the world, I'm not going anywhere," he promises, lifting my fingers to his lips and placing a kiss there. "It's been shit without you here. I've missed you so much. Skylar was really upset that you didn't reply to her or call her back."

"I just didn't want to talk to anyone involved with the MC," I admit. "But I know that she wasn't in on this, so I should have replied to her."

"She was really pissed at us," he says, puffing out a breath. "The clubhouse has been filled with tension, especially when Temper found out the truth. Skylar told him what happened, and he wasn't happy about it."

"At least someone was on my side," I grumble. I know he was trying to save his friend, this Trade guy, but it was at my expense. And yeah, he's changed his tune, but that doesn't change what happened.

"I hope that you can forgive me and know that I will always be honest with you and have your back from here on out. You can trust me, okay? And it might not feel like that right now, but I will prove it to you."

"Okay," I say softly, nodding. "Thank you for explaining everything to me."

"Thank you for listening," he replies, leaning back on his palms and looking up at the tree. "I used to come here as a kid and try to climb this tree."

"I was wondering why you chose this park." It obviously means something to him, if this is where he spent some of his childhood. I've noticed he rarely talks about growing up, or his family, so it's nice that he's opening up a little and speaking about these things.

"I come here to think sometimes," he admits, pointing to the lake. "And the little ducklings are kind of cute. I usually bring some bread to give to them."

"You don't really talk about your family," I decide to point out. To be fair, besides my sister, I've never really spoken about mine. I clearly never spoke about Dad and what happened with our family, and my mom's passing. I guess we both never opened up about our pasts, happier to focus on the now, and the new and exciting relationship we were building together.

"The MC is my family," he says, studying me. "I was an only child and my parents passed away in a car crash. None of my family wanted to take me in, so I was put in the system."

Another reason why he might have wanted to save Trade's kids from that.

Fuck.

"I lost my mom to cancer," I blurt out, staring down at my hands. "Ariel doesn't really like to talk about her, because she gets so upset, so Mom is kind of like the elephant in the room sometimes. We loved her more than anything, and losing her was the hardest thing we've both ever been through. And my dad, well…as I've said, we aren't close, and probably never will be."

"I'm sorry about your mom," he says, gently touching my arm to comfort me, but then backing away. It's like we don't know where we are anymore, and it's kind of awkward. I don't want him touching me, but at the same time I do. I want my space, but I also want him to keep pursuing me.

Basically, I don't know what the hell I want.

Which is why I need a little time to clear my head.

"Want to go down and walk around the lake?" I ask, standing up and offering him my hand for once.

He takes it and laughs as I try to pull him up, but then gives in and helps me by pushing to his feet and leading me toward the water.

"What else has been happening while I've been gone?" I ask, enjoying the fresh air and sunlight on my face.

"I've just been working," he replies, and I'm sure I hear him mutter, "And miserable," under his breath but I pretend that I don't. "So is your sister going to give me a beatdown?"

"She was going to throw her shoe at you if you stepped inside my house," I tell him, grinning. "And she would have, too. Baby in her arms and all."

He laughs softly. "Maybe I'll drop you home and take her for a ride to beg for her forgiveness, too."

"Not a bad idea," I reply in all seriousness. Ariel and Renny have to get along. She's my only family, and she's also my best friend. Her opinion does matter to me.

"I probably deserve the shoe," he admits after a few seconds. "I would have taken fifty shoes instead of you up and running away to Vegas. I thought about finding you, and making you listen to me, but I figured you'd come back when you were ready, and I knew I'd be waiting."

I did wonder while I was away if Renny would just show up at Ariel's door, taking control of the situation and demanding I listen to him.

"You said that I don't think any rules apply to me, that I can do whatever I want, so that's why I didn't follow you, because I didn't want to prove you right. You wanted space from me, so I let you have that, even though I didn't want to."

"Because it's not always about you," I remind him.

"I know that, but I also knew I had hurt you, and of course I wanted to fix it." He sighs, glancing over at me. "You're so far under my skin, and yeah, I guess it's been so long since I've actually cared about a woman that I haven't been handling it too well."

"So I'm like the splinter you never wanted but got anyway?" I ask, making him laugh out loud.

"You're a surprise splinter I never thought I'd be so lucky to find," he jokes back, then sobers. "I don't think you understand—I never connect to women like this. I mean, I'm nice to women, I love women, but I've never actually had an emotional and mental connection with one like this before."

That's kind of flattering, but also kind of sad.

"Guess you just never met the right one," I state, and he nods, agreeing.

"Nope, not until now, and then I went and fucked it all up," he admits, ducking his head. "You make me a better person, Izzy."

I'm glad that I do that, I really am, but does he make *me* a better person?

Or is he pulling me in the other direction?

Chapter Eighteen

"You were gone for a while," Ariel points out as I step in the door. "How did it all go?"

"Pretty well," I admit, giving her a rundown. She laughs when I tell her how he suggested taking her on a ride next so he can make her forgive him also.

"So are you going to forgive him?" she asks, no judgment in her tone.

I've always thought it was weak to forgive a man when he doesn't do right by you, but maybe it requires more strength. Maybe the right man just had to come along for me to want to fight for the relationship, I don't know.

"I said I needed some time to think," I tell her, but truth be told, I have softened toward him already. Not completely, but somewhat. If I decide to completely forgive him, we're going to have a lot of work to do, because my trust in him is shattered, and from now on I'm going to be second-guessing everything.

Is it worth it?

I don't know yet.

How I react now is going to set the standard for the future. I want those standards set very high, because I'm not going to tolerate any kind of lies or manipulation again.

Ariel hands me Mila. "Well, I'll support you no matter what, you know that. I'm going to have a shower and then finish unpacking the last of my boxes."

I sit down on my couch and cuddle the little sleeping bundle in my arms. I don't need to make any decisions now. I can take my time and listen to my head and my heart, and hopefully they'll both lead me in the right direction.

Hopefully.

When Skylar drops by the next day, it's a little awkward.

"Hey," I say, smiling and opening the door wider. "Come on in."

She steps inside and pulls me in for a big hug. "I'm so sorry about what happened. The men in the MC can be such assholes sometimes. I mean, it's good when you're on their side, because they will do anything to help you, even if it's morally questionable, but to be on the other end… You didn't deserve that, and if it makes you feel any better, I yelled at them all and snitched to Temper."

I laugh softly. "I know, Renny told me. Thank you for having my back and not being a part of the whole scheme. It makes me feel a little better about the whole thing."

She nods. "Will you come to the clubhouse with me? Temper wanted to have a chat with you."

"Sure," I agree, even though I've been feeling hesitant about ever going back there. I'm going to bite the bullet and get it over with. Besides, I have been wanting to speak with Temper, especially since Renny told me the whole story.

I lock my door and we walk to the clubhouse together. "Renny was miserable while you were gone," she says, sighing. "I know it doesn't change anything, but he was, and I think he knew how badly he had fucked up. The night you left, he got super drunk and I could tell he was regretting his life decisions."

I never wanted Renny to be miserable, even though I remember angry me saying something along those lines. But I do want him to know he can't manipulate people like that. The MC, like Skylar said, is obviously used to doing whatever they want as long as it benefits them, and not caring who gets caught up in the fallout, as long as it's not a Knight. While I love that they have their brotherhood and that they look out for each other and are loyal to one another, I'm a person who would never step on another human to get anywhere, no matter if I love them or not.

"Yeah, that was a rough night," I admit, glancing down at the road. "I think the hardest part was that mostly everyone knew and was in on it, so it just makes everything fake, you know? Every friendship, every conversation, every laugh."

"Saint truly does like you," she assures me. "He thinks you are perfect for Renny and he's happy for you both, so don't think that they were all pretending to be your friend. It wasn't just Renny who got attached to you. We all did."

It's quiet when we enter the clubhouse, and we find Temper sitting outside alone, tapping away on his phone. "Hey, Temper," Skylar says, letting him know we're here.

He lifts his head and flashes us a small smile. "Hey. Izzy, nice to see you back here."

"I'll make you both some coffee," Skylar says, making a quiet exit and leaving me and Temper alone.

"I wasn't sure if you would come here," he admits, studying me with wise brown eyes. Temper is an old soul, I think.

"I wasn't sure either," I reply in all honesty. "But I know that you didn't know, so you're one of the only people not on my shit list right now."

"They were trying to help me," he says, running his hand over his bald head. "I know it doesn't excuse anything for you, but it's hard be too angry at men who were trying to help your family."

"I heard your brother was arrested," I say. "I'm sorry to hear about his children."

"He gave up the life for his kids, and they must have seen him as a weak link and went after him. I don't know what they want, but I know that something is coming for us. A war is brewing. I just don't know how to help him."

"Who is 'they'?" I ask.

"We've made some enemies over the years," he admits, placing his phone down on the table. "I don't know if Renny or Skylar have told you, but last year we lost her father, Hammer. He was the president of the club before me."

"She did mention that, yes."

"He was a good man. The best man, actually, and losing him was hard," he says, throat working as he swallows. "But there could be backlash from what happened there, which is what I'm thinking it might be. The men must have thought the same and also wanted to help Trade out, especially since he hasn't had anything to do with the club in a few years now. It's a shitty feeling knowing something you did is affecting someone you love, someone innocent."

"So this is the con to the lifestyle, hey," I whisper, feeling for him. "And it's a big one."

He nods. "It is. But there's a reason the men didn't tell me about their plan for you, and it's because I never harm anyone who hasn't harmed me or the club. And you're a nice girl, and you're our neighbor, and I like how happy you make Renny."

I ignore the fact he admitted that he'd happily harm anyone who was an enemy of the Knights, which might even be how they've gotten themselves into this situation right now.

"I'm trying to get his kids back so they can stay with me," he continues. "But they're going to take one look at me and say no, which I'm preparing for, but at least I tried." The sadness in his tone kills me. "I just wanted to say I'm sorry for what they did to your car, and for lying, and trust me, I've had words with them all. I hope you can forgive Renny, because he's a good man at the end of the day and he will do anything for those he loves, which I'm sure you've found out."

Yeah, because I've been on the other end of it.

"My dad and I aren't close," I admit, feeling the need to explain myself. "He's not a great person, and I know that firsthand. I mean, he's not all bad, but if I ask for something like this, I know there are going to be huge ramifications. So I guess the question is, how badly do you want it?"

Am I really considering asking him? One conversation with Temper, and I'm ready to dive in and try and save a man I've never met so his kids, who I've also never met, can be reunited with him. The fucked-up thing is, I probably *can* save Trade. It's just that I know what my dad is going to ask of me in return, and I don't know if I'm willing to do that.

"You don't need to explain yourself. You owe us nothing. And I don't expect anything from you. They fucked up, all right? Don't put this on you," he says, frowning, then shaking his head. "You haven't done anything wrong."

"I know," I respond, and I do. "But I'm the type of person that will help if I can."

"This is a different level of help," he warns. "This isn't helping an old lady pay for her groceries or babysitting for a neighbor. Like you said, there will be ramifications, and if those fall on me, then that's fine. Hell, I've been dodging that shit for my whole life, but I'm not going to let anything fall on you. Especially for something that isn't your problem. You said the mayor isn't a good man? Then it's probably for the best, because we don't need any more problems right now."

Skylar returns with coffee, obviously having taken her time to give us some privacy and a moment to chat. I think about Temper's words, and I know that he's right. This isn't my problem, and bringing my dad into it will probably only bring out further problems down the line. However, it will also most likely get Temper's brother out of jail. I know the type of contacts Dad has. He could make it happen with just a phone call. Whether he will or not though, I can't tell, because he's extremely unpredictable.

"Thank you," I say to her, holding the mug in my hand. "So, what else have I missed in the last few weeks?"

"Nothing much. I think you going MIA and leaving was the big drama," Skylar admits, smirking. "Renny wasn't much fun to be around, and we were all yelling at each other—"

"I'm pretty sure it was only you doing the yelling, Sky," Temper deadpans, reaching over and squeezing her cheek. "And everyone else trying to calm you down."

"Well, can you blame me? You guys chased away the only other woman around here who isn't a—"

"No slut shaming, Sky." Temper cuts her off, amusement dancing in his eyes.

"The only other woman I'd consider a friend," she concludes, pulling her hair out of its ponytail and letting it fall down her back. "Not to mention I was left out of the loop, too. What other sneaky shit are you guys up to that I don't know about?"

"My worries exactly," I add, sharing a look with her. "I mean, I'm not involved in the club, but anything that affects Renny also affects me."

"It's true," Skylar agrees, nodding. "It's not an easy thing. I mean, I grew up with the MC, but I was always left in the dark about anything they would deem club business. And I know that it was to keep me safe and uninvolved, but it wasn't a nice feeling to be the only one who didn't know what was going on."

"We all wanted to protect you," Temper says to her in a gentle tone. "And you're family, but you're not a member. No women are. And now you're Saint's old lady, so it's up to you how much he wants to tell you. Most of the time, you're in the know."

"Because I proved myself," she states, looking Temper in the eye. "And because I was dragged into some shit. Member or not, I was there beside you all fighting my way out of it." She looks at me and adds, "Which was the day I ended up on your doorstep."

I've always wondered what happened that day. Skylar showed up, frantic and asking to use my phone, looking like she had fallen in a ditch or something. Of course I let her in and did what I could do for her in that moment, which wasn't much other than to let her make the call, and soon the rumble of motorcycles came for her. I don't know why she didn't go to the clubhouse, and I never asked her, but after seeing the gates out front, I'm thinking that maybe it was in lockdown and she couldn't get inside.

"Lucky for you I work from home and was there to let you in," I joke, lightening the mood. "I always thought about that day and hoped you were okay."

She reaches out and touches my hand.

And although we might never be members, maybe our own sisterhood is enough.

Chapter Nineteen

When Renny walks out and sees me, his eyes widen.

"Izzy," he murmurs, smiling. He's wearing a gray T-shirt today, and it looks good on him, clinging to his every muscle, yet not too tight, letting me imagine just how ripped he is underneath. I mean, I know the answer to that is very, but I wouldn't if I hadn't already seen him naked. "You hanging out here without me now?"

"Yep," I reply, popping the *P*. "Skylar dropped by and told me to come over, so here I am." I don't want him to think that I just invited myself over or something, because that would be awkward.

He kisses the top of my head and sits down next to me. "It's nice to see you here."

"Nice to be here." They must have been worried I would never return, too angry with everyone over what had happened. And if you had asked me before, I probably would have said the same thing. At the end of the day these guys were my friends, and they will always be my neighbors, unless I up and sell my house, so it feels good to speak with them all and make peace, no matter what happens with myself and Renny.

"Are you going to stay for dinner?" he asks, pulling

my chair closer to his. "You can bring your sister and niece over, too."

"What are we doing for dinner?" Temper asks, sounding confused.

"I think Renny's going to organize something because Izzy's here," Skylar whispers to Temper, making me laugh.

"Don't organize a dinner on my account," I tell Renny, grinning. Although it is sweet, and even nicer that he invited my family, it's very unnecessary.

"We can order pizza or something," he says on a shrug. "Or Chinese."

I know my sister won't want to come, especially not with a newborn, but I could send her a message inviting her so she feels included. They are her neighbors now also, but if she doesn't want to have anything to do with the MC, that is also okay, and very much up to her.

"Yeah, let's order Chinese," Skylar says, rubbing her hands together. "It's been ages since I've had any dumplings. I love the ones that have the soup in them."

"It's Izzy's choice," Renny pointedly tells her, scowling at Skylar.

Don't try and steal my thunder, I mouth to her, making her laugh out loud.

"Chinese is good," I tell him, smiling.

Eventually Saint and Dee show up, along with another two men I've never seen before. "Who are they?" I ask Renny, eying the two young, attractive men.

"New recruits," he replies, scowling. "Why?"

"I've never seen them before," I explain, rolling my eyes at him for obviously assuming I was checking them out. "What are their names?"

His lips tighten. "I think you better stop looking in

their direction or they're about to get kicked out of the fucking club."

I look to Skylar with wide eyes, only to find her looking back at me with a similar expression.

What the fuck? I mouth to her.

"He's jealous," she replies, lip twitching.

I pause, and then ask, "Seriously, though, what are the new guys' names?"

Ignoring the growling noise that comes from Renny, Temper introduces me to the prospects: Crow, who is tall, lean and blond and blue-eyed, with neck tattoos peeping out of his Hawaiian shirt, and Chains, whose dark hair and eyes are almost menacing.

"Nice to meet you both," I tell them, smiling politely.

"You, too," Crow says, winking at me. "I can tell that I'm going to like it around here."

Renny steps in front of me, staring Crow down. "She's mine. Don't even breathe in her direction, because I will end you."

Crow throws his hands up. "Noted. Just being polite."

Even after everything that has happened, there's no way I'd have eyes for anyone other than Renny, especially in his clubhouse. Tugging on his hand, quietly telling him to cut it out, I pull him away from poor Crow and lead him into the kitchen.

"I wasn't checking them out, I was being polite and curious," I quietly tell him, frowning. "I'm supposed to be the one who has trust issues with you, not the other way around."

"I didn't like the way he was looking at you," he grumbles, opening the fridge and getting us two bottles of water. "And he needs to know now that he has no fuckin' chance, either."

"He was just being nice," I reply. "He's new here, he's going to be nice to everyone."

"Chains hasn't been nice to anyone," he fires back, smirking. "Crow should be more like him."

Stepping closer to him, I look up at him. "I know we're in a weird place right now, but that doesn't mean that my eyes have started wandering, all right? Especially around your friends and family. I'd never do that to you."

"I know," he admits, tucking my hair back behind my ear. "The thought of you with someone else just kills me, all right? And yeah, I don't even know if we're together or not, I don't think you even know either, so I'm a little on edge right now."

"I'm here, aren't I?" I say, resting my hand on his chest. "I don't know what's going to happen, but that has to mean something."

Dee enters into the kitchen, stopping in his tracks when he sees us. "Can I speak to her?" he asks Renny, avoiding my gaze.

Renny glances down at me, silently asking if that's okay.

"Sure." I nod.

He hands me the water and then leaves, eying Dee on the way out.

"I just wanted to say that I'm sorry," Dee starts, pulling a chair out and sitting on it. "I'm the one who found out that you were the mayor's daughter, who came up with the plan, and I'm the one who put pressure on Renny when he called it all off."

"Yes, I know, but you aren't the one I was falling in love with, so you telling me these things doesn't hurt me as much as Renny ever being a part of the whole thing,"

I admit, sitting down next to him. "I appreciate the apology, I really do."

"You're a gracious woman, Izzy."

"Did you guys even need to go to Vegas, or was that just an excuse to get close to me?" I ask, something I just realized I've never asked Renny.

"We were planning on doing a trip to visit the Vegas Chapter of the Knights," he admits, wincing. "But did we need to leave right then and there? No, we didn't."

"I thought as much," I say, taking a deep breath.

"Yeah, it's fucked up, I know. But for the record, Renny made the right call."

He stands up and kisses my forehead, then leaves the kitchen. Taking a deep breath, I lean my head back and try to pull myself together. The men are so forward and confrontational, and I know it's a good thing to put everything out in the open so we can move on, but it's also quite draining and a lot to take in.

The food arrives, and we all sit at the outside table and eat together, chatting and laughing like nothing has changed.

Except it has, and I don't know what's going to happen next.

When the name *Dad* flashes on my phone a few days after, curiosity has me picking it up this time. "Hello?" I say.

"Isabella?" he replies in greeting. "How have you been, daughter? I've called you a few times now, but you haven't answered."

"I know," I tell him. "I've been busy with work, and helping Ariel with Mila."

He goes silent at the mention of his first grandchild,

the one he's yet to meet. "I'm sure Ariel told you about what we discussed the last time I contacted her."

"Yes. Someone saw me on the back of a motorcycle, and somehow thought it was their business to tell you," I say, rolling my eyes. "And you think it will be a bad look for you, so you rang to tell me to only take transport with four wheels?"

"Cute," he grumbles. "It has nothing to do with what looks bad for me, Isabella. I'm worried about you. Who is this man that you've been seen with? Is he your boyfriend? I heard he was wearing a cut, that means he's part of an MC."

"That's a lot of assumptions you're making there," I say. "Why, what does it matter if he's a biker or not? I can't even remember the last time I saw you—was it last Christmas? Or maybe the one before? I don't know. I don't see how what I'm doing with my life affects you at all, Dad. Nobody even knows we're related."

"That's what you think," he replies, sighing heavily. "I'm still your father, and of course I care about what's going on in your life."

I go silent, my mind running. "I have a question for you, Dad."

"What is it?" he asks, sounding suspicious.

"If I had a friend who was in jail, is there any way you would be able to get him released as a favor to you? He didn't do what they've accused him of."

I know how bad that sounds. Everyone says they didn't do what they've been accused of, and I'm just going by the word of others—others who have lied to me before. But my gut is saying that Temper was being honest, that this Trade guy has been put in a shit place to get back at the MC.

"What did this *friend* do?" he asks. "And who are these people you are keeping company with these days?"

"They found drugs in his house," I reply, ignoring his other question.

"I mean, I could see what I could do, yes," he replies, but then says no more.

"Yes or no, Dad. Just how powerful are you?" I challenge.

One thing about my dad, he has a huge ego, and he doesn't like it one bit when you question him.

"Yes, of course I can," he replies, scorn filling his tone. "Why should I, though?"

"You're still my father, aren't you?" I ask, using his words against him.

He's silent for a few moments as he thinks. "I can get your friend out of jail, but if I do, I want you to lose the biker."

I knew this was going to happen.

I just knew it.

These are the ramifications, and they are going to solely fall on me.

To save Trade, I'm going to have to give up Renny.

I know how important family is, and if Ariel was in trouble, or Mila, and someone could help them, I'd want them to do that. Sibling love and loyalty mean everything to me, and if I can help Trade, I want to do that.

I asked Temper just how badly he wanted it, and he said he'd do anything as long as the consequences fell on him, but they're not going to. They're going to fall on me, and on Renny.

And I need to decide what I'm going to do.

Chapter Twenty

"He said *what*?" Ariel asks, pacing. "He wants you to cut all contact with Renny? Does he know that you live down the road from him? It's going to be kind of hard to do that even if you wanted to, which is why you faced your fears and jumped on a damn plane."

"I know. And Dad's never been to my house, but he has to know where I live, right?" I ask, wrinkling my nose. "My dad has never been to my house, how sad is that?"

"Pretty sad," she muses, sitting down next to me and sighing. "How are these your life problems right now?"

"I have no idea," I groan, covering my face with my hands. "And how is he going to ensure I stick to my word? I could just not ride with Renny, but it's not like he'd know who is going to be in my bed, or who I'm spending my free time with."

"Maybe he doesn't care as long as you're not out in the open where people can see and tie it back to him?" she guesses, resting her cheek on her palm. "I don't know. Maybe he has some secret ulterior motive we have no idea about, and he's going to drop it on us like a bombshell."

"Like when he left Mom for another woman?" I add, pursing my lips.

"Yeah, like that."

"You just never know with him," I agree. "I'm just going to think on it for now. Maybe I should run it by Renny and see what he thinks? I don't know. Bringing Dad into the mix is dangerous, he's such a wild card, but after hearing about Trade…"

I feel bad for a man I don't even know, and he means something to the MC, to Temper. I'd like to help them and his children.

"What do you think I should do?" I ask my big sister.

"I think you should speak to Renny," she replies, nodding. "Yeah, I think that's the best bet. Don't try to be some martyr and just do this and not tell him. He will be pissed. And I think you should just be honest and work with him, not against him."

Work with him.

I could do that.

"You're right," I whisper. "I need to speak to him."

I could have just agreed, not told Renny, and then he would have been left confused and hurt when I withdrew from him, which isn't fair to him. He's invested in me, and I don't want to hurt him, but maybe I can save Trade and make it work with Renny, too?

Can I have my cake and eat it, too, or is my dad going to expect something like this and be one step ahead of me?

I stand up. "I'm going to go over there now. Do you want to come?"

"No, I'm going to stay here and watch movies," she says, smiling at me. "I'll leave the excitement up to you."

"Okay, I'll be back soon," I promise. "How do you feel about us getting a guard dog? I feel like with everything going on, we're going to have to up the security here. Renny said he can sort it out for us."

Although there hasn't been a direct threat to us, and there might never be, I'd rather be safe than sorry.

"I think that's a great idea," she says, brow furrowing. "Between Dad, Merve and the MC, we never know what the hell is going to happen around here."

"I've wanted a dog for so long," I admit, smiling widely. "You have no idea. How do you feel about a Boerboel? They are huge, so cute and pretty much bred for protection."

"I knew you were going to want one of those," she says, smiling. "I'm happy with whatever you want."

"How did you know?"

She rolls her eyes. "You've mentioned them a few times. And I remember everything you say."

"Oh. Well, you know what they say, an elephant never forgets."

I leave her laughter behind in the house and jog down to the clubhouse. I send Renny a message to let him know I'm coming over to chat on the way, then enter through the open gate and knock on the door.

Temper opens it, inviting me in when he sees me. "Is Renny here?" I ask.

"He's in the gym," he says, pointing me in the right direction.

"Thanks."

He's lifting weights when I step into their makeshift gym, which is actually a really cool spot and has everything they could need. Renny is alone in the room, shirtless, and in nothing but a pair of black basketball shorts, his arms moving up and down with each lift.

I wait until he's finished before speaking, not wanting to scare him and have him drop the bar on his head.

"Need a spotter?" I ask him, my heart skipping a beat at his smile as he sees me.

"Isn't this a nice surprise?" he murmurs, taking me in.

My eyes can't help but roam his body, especially his abs. None of the men I've been with before have had a six pack, and all I want to do is run my tongue down it once more.

He strolls over to me, grabbing his towel along the way. "Probably not a good idea to look at me like that."

I kind of think it's a great idea actually, especially since it's been weeks since we last slept together, and with him looking like that… I want him.

"Why is that?" I ask him, placing my hand on his sweaty chest and taking a step closer to him.

He makes a soft growling sound and leads me to his room, locking the door behind us and then taking us into the bathroom. He turns the shower on, drops his shorts and briefs and stands there in all of his glory.

"You going to join me?" he asks, heat in his gaze.

I pull down my leggings and lift off my white top, throwing them on the ground and leaving me standing there in black cotton. I didn't exactly plan for us to have sex, so I didn't put anything racy on, but the way he's looking at me makes me feel like the sexiest woman alive.

When the bra and panties join the pile on the floor, I step into the warm water with him, and before you know it I'm back in his arms, his lips on mine, our bodies pressed together, droplets of water falling all over us. He lifts me up and pushes my back against the glass screen, hands on my ass, squeezing and kneading each globe.

When he pulls back and looks me in the eye, the emotion there is nearly my undoing. He needs this as much as I do.

Cupping his face, I kiss him again slowly at first, but then harder, deeper, and when he presses his cock against my sex, I'm more than ready for him. Making a sound of encouragement in his throat, he slides the tip in, slowly, gently. He has all the control in this position, and I'm so hot and horny right now that I just want him to fuck me, but he plays it out, kissing my neck and taking his time, teasing me.

"Renny," I plead, which must work on him, because he thrusts inside me, both of us moaning at the same time, then continues to slowly work himself in and out, all the while kissing me, touching me and stroking me. It's not long before he makes me come, scoring my nails down his back and whispering his name as I do so. Lifting me up higher, he moves against me faster, deeper, until he finishes inside me.

"Fuck," he grits out, body jerking.

Once he's done, he kisses me again, pushing my wet hair off my face and gently rubbing his hands down my arms and back up to my cheeks. "I missed you."

"I could tell," I reply, smiling against his lips. "I missed you, too."

He places me back down on the floor, my legs feeling like jelly, and then squirts some soap into his hands and gently rubs it all over my body. I let my eyes fall closed and just enjoy it. It's been a long few weeks without being touched like this.

"I'm glad you dropped by," he says into my ear, making me grin.

"Me, too. I did come here for a reason, though, you know, other than to come."

He chuckles softly. "I thought as much."

We finish up in the shower, dry ourselves and jump in bed before I tell him what I came here to tell him.

"So your dad will help Trade so long as you stop seeing me?" he repeats, jaw going tight. "Over my fuckin' dead body."

"And I don't even know if he will keep his word, which is the same thing he could say for me, so it's a pretty iffy deal. But it's all we have right now if you want to get Trade out of jail as soon as possible," I tell him, shrugging. "I don't know. You guys need to let me know what you want to do."

"I'm not giving you up for anybody," he states, pulling me against him. "If your dad doesn't like that you're with a biker, too bad for him, because it's too late."

"Too late for what?"

"Too late for either of us to walk away from each other," he says, rolling on top of me. "I know you're still angry at me, but come on, Izzy. I think we both know we're in too deep now. I've fallen in love with you. I can't just walk away and I'm not going to let you do the same, especially when it's not you who wants to do so."

"You're in love with me?" I ask, searching his gaze.

"Yes, I am," he replies, brown eyes gentling. "Very much."

Am I in love with Renny?

I think I am, but I'm not one hundred percent sure, or maybe I am but my pride won't allow me to say it yet. We're supposed to be on some break while I figure out if we can be together, but we've already broken that by sleeping together anyway. I don't regret being with him, not one bit, but it doesn't change anything.

I open my mouth to speak but he shakes his head,

stroking my hair. "You don't have to say anything. Are you going to sleep here tonight?"

I nod. "Yeah, I better message Ariel."

It wouldn't feel nice to sleep with him then not stay the night. I've missed his cuddles more than anything, and spending the night wrapped up in him sounds perfect.

I send her a quick message, then lie back down with Renny.

"We'll talk to Temper about this whole thing tomorrow," he says, sighing. "We'll find a solution, okay? One that doesn't involve you walking away from me. I'm glad that you came to me and didn't consider doing it."

I go silent, because I did consider it, but I'm glad that I didn't go through with it because it would have been silly. I'm not going to lose the man I love because my dad doesn't think it will look good for his image.

Love.

Shit. I *am* in love with him.

I decide to keep it to myself until the right time makes itself known, until we are in a good place again.

For now, it can be my secret.

Chapter Twenty-One

"Well, at least we know the mayor's view on bikers," Saint muses, turning to look at Temper. "Thoughts, prez?"

"His request is stupid," Temper replies, pacing up and down the kitchen with a scowl on his face. "I think I need to speak to him, man to man. Do you think you could arrange that for us, Izzy?"

"Sure."

"That's where your involvement in this will end, though," he says, pausing in his steps to look at me. "I don't want you to give anything or lose anything, all right? You've done enough to help the MC, and because of how this whole thing came about, I don't want you feeling used in any way, shape or form."

I open my mouth, but he cuts me off before I even say anything. "And I hope you didn't even consider taking any deal he offered you, because this isn't your problem, it's mine." I decide to nod, agreeing, and to let him continue. "I'm going to speak to him and see what I can do to get him in our court."

"I'm going to spend the day working on the clubhouse security, and Izzy's security at her house," Renny inserts, looking at all of the men. "I think we need to hope for the best, but be prepared for the worst."

I know there's something they're not telling me, and I think it has to do with Hammer's death. Is someone coming after them? Temper said they have enemies, but who, and why?

"All right," Temper mutters, then turns to say something to Skylar that makes no sense to me. "Do we have eyes on your mom?"

"She's on the farm," Skylar tells him.

The little meeting ends, and Renny escorts me back home, joining me on my walk of shame, wearing last night's clothes. "I'm going to get a guard dog."

"That's a good idea," he agrees. "Temper suggested getting a few rottweilers or something for the clubhouse, but I know that if the cops step inside and the dogs are barking at them, they'll probably just shoot them, and then we'll all be devastated."

"So you didn't get dogs so the cops can't kill them? That's really sad." I hope no cops ever come to my house, although I don't know why they'd have reason to, considering I've never done anything illegal in my life. Still, I guess I'll now be guilty by association from here on out.

"I can see why your dad wouldn't want you to be with me," he says quietly, eyes down. "But know that the club and I will protect you with all we have, and that we will do everything in our power to make sure that nothing touches you or your family."

"I know," I assure him. "I'm not dwelling on what he said, trust me. I don't need his approval to be with who I want to be with. If he were a different person and we had a close relationship, maybe, but he isn't and we don't, so you don't have to worry that his opinion will ever make me change my mind about you. I knew exactly who you were before we started dating, and I'm never going to ask you to change anything about you. I mean, besides the whole lying thing."

"I know I deserve it, but man, you know how to hold a grudge," he grumbles, taking my hand as I walk along the curb. "But I'm glad that his comments don't have you running away. Not that you'd get very far, considering you're just down the road."

"Dad jokes, hey?" I tease, smirking. "Nope, I haven't run since high school, so I don't think you have to worry about that."

We stop at my front door, and I give him a hungry kiss before we enter.

"I'm home!" I call out, placing my bag and keys on the table near the door and heading to the kitchen.

"Hey," Ariel replies from the couch. "I'm guessing your vagina trumped your grudge-holding skills, eh?"

I cover my face with my hands. "I probably should have told you that Renny is here with me, coming to up our security game in the house."

I chance a look at his expression, but he's just amused, eyes dancing.

"My comment is still valid," she replies, coming into the kitchen with Mila in her arms, her eyes narrowed. "Renegade."

"Ariel," he says, smiling at her full-naming him. "How are you?" He glances down and adds, "Just making sure you're not wearing any shoes that you can throw at me."

Ariel's lip twitches. "Not too bad, and yourself?" she replies, as I hold out my arms for Mila.

"I'm okay," he says. "Going to upgrade all the locks and install a security camera in here."

"Isn't she the cutest?" I ask Renny, introducing him to Mila.

He glances down at her and grins. "She is the cutest baby I've ever seen, I think." He then proceeds to baby talk to her. "Hello, Mila. Aren't you just gorgeous? You look like a mini version of your mom and aunty."

Ariel and I share a look while he continues to fuss, eventually taking her from my arms and holding her. He looks really good with a baby. A little too good—my ovaries are about to burst.

"Well, I've forgiven him," Ariel whispers, watching him with her daughter. "And also can he babysit, so me and you can go out to the movies or something? Because that would be great."

"I love kids," he says, gently rocking Mila. There's something about seeing a big, built, sexy, tattooed man holding a little vulnerable baby, and him being so gentle and sweet to her, that is really, really sexy.

He hands Mila back to Ariel with a smile, then turns back to me. "I'm going to check the house, then go and get what I need."

"Sounds good. I'll make us all some lunch."

Renny does the recon while I make some nachos and guacamole. Flashbacks of us last night keep hitting me, and the fact that we had sex twice more after in the shower doesn't make me want him any less right now.

Will that ever go away?

I hope not.

I can't believe that I've unconsciously decided to give him a second chance, my actions speaking louder than my words.

I just can't let go of him, not yet.

Maybe not ever.

"Now when someone comes to the door, we don't even have to get up, how good is it? We can see who is there on our phones and decide whether we want to answer it or not," I say to Ariel, my feet up on the coffee table as we watch a movie together. Renny installed the cameras, upgraded all of the locks and blocked off one side of the house so no one can enter from that area. Something about a controlled setting. The cameras come with two screens, one for Ariel and one for me, which are portable, so we can put them wherever we want and have a constant stream of everything happening on our property.

"I know. No more dealing with salesmen," she agrees, tossing some popcorn in her mouth. "And less walking around for no reason."

"When we get the puppy, we're going to have to do daily walks, though," I tell her. "It will be cute, little family outings. We can put Mila in her stroller and walk down to the local dog park."

"I suppose I could lose some of my baby weight," she says, wrinkling her nose.

I eye her. "You don't have any baby weight. You look exactly the same." And she does. Yeah, she has the slightest stomach, but it just looks like she ate a whole pizza or something. Even my stomach does that. "I'd totally be rocking the mom bod if I were you. This is the time to let yourself go."

She laughs and throws a pillow at me. "Maybe you'll be pregnant soon, especially with the way Renny was looking at you today, like he wanted to eat you whole. I felt like I was watching the beginning of a porno. He was the handyman fixing shit, and you were the housewife, cooking lunch and watching him."

I blink slowly a few times. "Do me a favor and never say anything like that ever again. Ew."

She just laughs, and it's nice to watch and hear her do

so. She has been so stressed lately about Merve, and the lawyer appointments she made, which he never showed up to or responded to. We have no idea where he is or what he's going to do, but at least he doesn't know where Ariel lives now. I guess he will contact her when he wants to, as she still has the same number.

"Maybe it's just because the last time I had sex was when I got pregnant with Mila," she muses, continuing with the oversharing. "And it wasn't even good sex. Merve isn't exactly what I would call a generous lover."

"Why does that not surprise me one bit?" I reply in a dry tone. "You were always way too good for him. I mean, I'm not going to say I wish he was never born, because then we wouldn't have Mila, but what the hell were you thinking?"

She sighs heavily and presses pause on the movie, giving me her full attention. "He's good-looking, we all know that, it's the one thing he does have. But I don't know, he was kind of charming back then, and had the whole bad boy thing going on. I mean, come on, you know the allure. Look at who you're dating."

"Hey, Renny is nothing like Merve. He's funny, kind, smart and *really* generous in bed. And if he had a kid, I'm sure he'd be a great dad." Also unlike Merve. "And he's smoking hot. You should see him naked," I add, giggling.

"I'd rather not," Ariel deadpans, lip kicking up at the corners. "Does he have any hot friends?"

I arch my brow. "Yeah, he does. Bikers in all shapes, ages and sizes. Come to the clubhouse and let me show you."

She unpauses the movie and continues to stare at the screen. "No way, at least not now. I just had a baby—I don't have time for a man right now. Mila is my priority."

"You might not have time for a man but surely in a few months or so you'll have time for a little penis," I reply, snickering to myself.

"I don't want to have time for a little penis," she replies, smirking. "Only big ones, please."

There's nothing better than having a sister. You can say whatever the hell you want, no matter how uncensored or immature, and she won't bat an eyelash. She'll just feed off you and keep the conversation going.

No judgment, no sensitivity, just pure, unconditional love.

The best kind.

Chapter Twenty-Two

I'm pretending to work the next day, but really am just scrolling through my social media when I see a post pop up about a dog someone is giving away because apparently they don't have time for him anymore. If nobody wants him they are going to hand him into the shelter.

"People are such assholes," I mutter to myself, looking at the picture of the sad-looking staffy-Rhodesian ridgeback mix.

"Why are people assholes?" Ariel asks, stepping into the living room with the mop in her hands.

I show her the post. "They are giving away this two-year-old dog, and look at his little face."

She looks at it and then back at me. "Want to go have a look at him?"

I grin, stand up and get changed.

Twenty minutes later we're at this family's house, and we see Shadow chained up in the backyard, looking miserable.

"Why is he chained?" I ask the man, unable to hide my disapproval.

He glances at me from the corner of his eye. "He barks at the slightest noise or when anyone walks past, and he also tries to jump the fence."

"Do you exercise him?" I dare to ask. Maybe if he went for a walk or something, he wouldn't be trying to escape to take himself for a walk.

"He pulls on the lead," is all the man replies, so I'm going to take that as a no.

"How is he with kids?" Ariel asks, Mila in her arms.

"Great. He loves our kids," the man says, sounding genuine about that fact. "He's a good guard dog but loyal to his family. I trust him with my three for sure."

"You wait here," I say to Ariel, just in case Shadow jumps up on her or something while she has Mila. "I'll suss him out."

Ariel agrees and waits by the car, while I enter this man's garden through the side gate. I pretend I don't see the marijuana plants and head straight for Shadow, who barks when he sees me, but stops when the man says, "It's okay, Shadow."

Then he starts to wag his tail as he runs over, all but jumping in my arms and licking my face. "Aren't you a good boy?" I say, patting the ridge of hair on his back. He looks more staffy, but has the coloring and markings that I've seen on purebred Rhodesian ridgebacks, just with a little white on his chest. He is beautiful, and one look into those brown eyes and I'm in love.

"Do you want to come home with me?" I ask him.

He licks my cheek.

"I'm going to take that as a yes," I say, laughing as he licks me more.

Looking at his owner, I say, "I'd love to take him, and I'll make sure he has a permanent, loving home."

Leading Shadow to the car, he jumps right in the front with me, which is good so he can't lick Mila in the back.

Ariel looks over me and smiles. "He's so cute! Welcome to the family, Shadow."

That evening, when Renny comes over, Shadow runs to the door, barking and growling his head off.

"It's okay, Shadow," I say, using the same command his previous owner used.

He calms instantly and sits, looking at the door. I open it to see a confused Renny, who glances down at Shadow and then back up at me. "You got a dog?"

I nod. "This is Shadow. Isn't he great?"

Renny steps in and Shadow just eyes him. "Is he going to bite me?"

Wrinkling my nose, I glance down at my new best friend. "I don't actually know—we only got him a few hours ago, so I can't make any promises. Also I'm pretty sure he was used as a guard dog to protect the drugs the man had growing in his garden."

"Do you trust him around Mila?" Renny asks, closing the door behind him, not taking his eyes off Shadow. "Did you think this through or did you just rush in to save some dog from a drug dealer?"

"He's great with kids," I tell him, frowning. "We introduced him to Mila, and he just sniffed her and loved her. It was fine. He grew up around children."

Renny takes a step closer to me and Shadow growls a little, so I lean down and say, "It's fine, Shadow. Come on in, just ignore him. I'm sure he will warm up to you." Taking Renny's hand, I pull him into the living room. "We love the security cameras, by the way. Thank you so much for installing them for us. And with Shadow, we already feel so much safer."

"You're welcome," he replies, sitting down. "Did you speak to your dad?"

"Yeah, I called him just before, and he said he'd have a meeting, but Temper has to go to him. I gave him Temper's number so tell him to keep his phone handy," I say, shrugging. "I don't know how this is going to play out, but I could tell he was intrigued by meeting the president of the Knights of Fury MC."

And also highly unimpressed that I knew Temper well enough to be facilitating this meeting, but that's another story.

"Okay, well, that's a good sign," Renny murmurs, eying Shadow, who is sitting right in front of him, staring. "I'm your dad, why are you looking at me like that?" he says to him.

"You're not his dad. We aren't married anymore, remember?" I tease, smirking.

"Just because we aren't legally married right now doesn't mean we won't be again one day," he fires back, shrugging.

"I'd like a proper proposal this time around, and all the trimmings," I tell him. "Not a wedding that I can't even remember."

I glance up to see Ariel standing in front of us wide-eyed. "What?"

Oh, fuck.

Cringing, I open my mouth, close it, then open it again. "Renny and I got drunk and married in Vegas and I didn't tell you because I knew you'd kill me. But don't worry, now it's all annulled so no one needs to ever speak about it again. We can all just pretend it didn't happen."

"Isabella Marie Johnson," she growls, shaking her head. "You are a walking cliché and I can't believe you didn't tell me this! And you," she grits out, pointing at Renny. "How did you let that happen?"

"Are you angrier that I did it, or that I didn't tell you?" I ask, wincing.

Green eyes narrow. "Both! I'm actually going to kill you, Izzy. Mom is probably rolling in her grave right now."

Okay, ouch, that was a low blow.

She storms off all dramatically, stomping like a baby elephant, while I sit there groaning. "That went better than I thought it was going to. Imagine if it wasn't annulled, she actually would have killed me."

"Really?" Renny asks, confusion all over his expression. "You thought it would be worse than that?"

"Yeah." I nod. "I think I got off lightly. We got married, Renny. It's kind of a big deal, you know?"

"Oh, I know," he whispers, standing up. "I'm going to go and talk to her."

"Are you sure you want to do that? I usually let her cool down before I try and speak to her."

Which, I think, is the smart thing to do. Otherwise people say all kinds of things in anger, and words are something that, once spoken, cannot be taken back.

"Yeah, I'm sure," he says, following Ariel.

"Your dad has big balls," I whisper to Shadow, who gives me a head tilt in response. I pat him and try to listen for any yelling, but the house remains quiet, so it must not be going too badly. When Renny resurfaces it's with Ariel by his side, who studies me for a few seconds, a scowl still settled firmly on her pretty face, but she says, "I can't believe you didn't tell me."

"I didn't want to see the disappointment on your face that I see right now," I admit, biting my lip. "And it's all sorted now, Ariel. We handled it."

"And I've never done something stupid? You've seen

my baby daddy," she says, rolling her eyes. "We all make mistakes, and yes, I will yell at you and tell you that you're stupid, because that's what big sisters do, but after that I'm going to be there for you to help you get out of said stupid situation."

"I was going to just hide it under the rug," I admit, exhaling deeply. "I didn't know Renny and I would start dating, I didn't know any of this would happen, and I was just going to pretend it didn't happen. And if I told you that was going to make it very, very real."

She sits down next to me and gives me a big hug. "Don't censor me from anything, okay? You know I'll always get over it."

"Okay, the next time I get married, I'll make sure that you're there," I promise her, grinning.

Renny mutters something, but I don't hear him. "What did you say?"

"Nothing," he replies, flashing me his teeth. "Aren't you happy everything is out in the open now?"

"Yeah, I am. I actually forgot that I didn't tell her, to be honest, which is obviously why I brought it up without even thinking about it," I admit, shaking my head. "All the other stuff that has been going on has kind of overpowered the marriage debacle. Who would have thought?"

"Not me," Ariel replies, standing up when she hears Mila cry. "Never would have thought that you'd be married before me."

She leaves the room and Renny sits back down next to me.

"What did you say to her, Mr. Smooth-talker?" I ask, kissing him softly on his cheek, his stubble pricking me.

"The truth," he replies, kissing my lips. "I'll go tell

Temper about the meeting. What are your plans for the rest of the day?"

"I'm going to buy Shadow some new things, like a bed, bowl, lead and collar, and then take him for a walk. Apparently he doesn't do too well on the lead, but I think he'll be fine."

"Do you want me to come with you?" he asks, giving Shadow a dubious look.

"Yeah, that would be nice. We don't know if he's good with other dogs. I might get a muzzle until we know what we're working with here."

"Probably a good idea," Renny agrees, reaching out to pat him.

Shadow doesn't react negatively at all, he just lifts his head up for more love.

"See, he's a big softy, he just looks tough," I say, watching the two of them interact. "He's a great guard dog, too. He will bark if someone he doesn't know even comes near the property."

I can see Renny already warming up to him, especially when he pats the couch and lets Shadow sit next to him on it.

"Is he allowed on the couch?" he asks me afterward, looking a little sheepish.

"Yeah, why not? He's a member of the family now, and I'm pretty sure he's spent most of his life on a chain." But all that is over for him now, and I'm going to make sure he's the most happy, spoiled pooch around.

We go to update Temper, then head to the shops to pick up Shadow's new belongings. When we return home with his new lead and collar, he starts jumping, so excited.

"We should probably avoid the dog park until we know what he's like," I tell Renny, stepping out the front door.

Shadow begins to pull straight away, almost yanking my arm off, so Renny takes the lead and lets him pull until he gets tired of it. Only when he relaxes does he start the walk, and although he does pull a little and walk on each side of us, getting himself tangled, he's not as bad as he was made out to be. He ignores the other humans and dogs as we pass them, and I think he's just happy to be included and getting some fresh air.

"He's a good boy," Renny finally admits on our way home. "The pulling thing we can fix; he just needs a little training and patience."

"I'm so glad I went on a whim and got him," I say, holding Renny's hand and smiling up at him. "He fits into our family so well—come on, admit it."

And I helped save him, which is much better than forking out thousands for a puppy.

Adopt, don't shop.

"He does. We'll have to bring him to the clubhouse so everyone can meet him."

"Sounds good."

We head home and I catch up on some work while Renny cooks us all dinner.

We might not be your normal family, but we definitely are becoming one.

Chapter Twenty-Three

"There's no way I can concentrate knowing Temper is sitting somewhere in a meeting with Dad right now," I say to Ariel, tapping my foot nervously. "What if it's a setup? Could you imagine? What if he plants some bullshit on Temper and now he's in jail with his brother?"

"Temper is the president of an MC—I doubt he'd have to plant anything," Ariel reminds me, arching her brow. "These aren't choir boys you've decided to align yourself with."

"I don't need your logic right now," I groan, covering my face with my hands. "It's Dad. Dad always has a plan."

And they say you end up with someone just like your father. Great.

Renny always has a plan, too.

"I'm sure Temper didn't get to where he is without a plan, too. Have some faith," she says, bringing me some lunch. "Here, eat. Food is always the answer."

I take a few bites of the sandwich she made, but I keep checking my phone for updates from Renny about how the meeting went. Is Dad going to demand that Renny leaves me alone? What if that's the only thing he wants from the MC? I don't want to lose Renny, and I know he won't give me up, but we still need a plan to get Trade out of this pickle he's found himself in.

A knock at the door makes Shadow lose his shit, and my eyes move straight to the screen to see who it is. A cute, petite, middle-aged lady stands there, holding a piece of paper.

"There's a lady at the door," I tell Ariel. "Shadow!"

He comes back to me, which is a good thing, and I hold on to his collar while Ariel answers the door. I hear a muted conversation, and then she returns with a flyer. "Just some lady looking for her dog."

"Aw no," I say, frowning. "I haven't seen any dogs roaming around here."

"Me either, but we can keep an eye out." She hands me the picture, and it's of a golden Labrador.

"What a gorgeous dog." I look down at Shadow. I'd be devastated if he got away and I had no idea where he was or what had happened to him. "Maybe we could help her look for him," I suggest.

Before she can answer, my phone rings with Renny's name popping up on my screen. "Hello?"

"Hey, I'm coming over now," he says.

"Okay." He says goodbye and hangs up, and I share a look with Ariel. "I guess we're about to find out how much of an asshole our dad is."

"I hope you're not expecting much from him," she replies, kissing the top of Mila's dark head. "Because you know he lets us down, every damn time."

I know, but still.

How did we turn out so different from him?

Surely there's some good in him?

When Renny steps through the door with Temper, I'm a little surprised to see the president in my space.

Still, I make sure he feels welcome, introducing him to my sister and niece and telling them to come in and sit down. My mom once told me that only people with class introduce others to each other, and that line has always stuck with me.

"So he said he'd help me get Trade out and get his kids back," Temper starts with, cracking his knuckles.

"And what did he ask for in return?" I ask him, brows drawing together.

"At first he said all he wanted was the MC to stay away from you," he admits, glancing over at Renny. "But I pointed out that that is impossible to govern, and impossible in general. So he came back with a counteroffer."

"And what is it?" I ask, looking at Ariel. What does our darling father want from the Knights?

"We owe him a marker, no questions asked. One he can call in at any time," he explains, crossing his arms over his chest. "He mentioned that he's been getting some threats and a little bit of blackmail, and apparently we have a mutual enemy, so I think he'll want our help with something to do with that. But he just doesn't know what that is yet."

"Does that make you allies?" I ask, surprised at this turn of events. "Your enemy's enemy is your friend, right?"

"I wouldn't go that far," Temper replies, frowning. "But yeah, for the time being, I think we're on the same level with everything. He's working on getting Trade out right now."

Feeling a little suspicious, I ask, "So, you're saying things are looking up, and everything might work out?"

"We can only hope," Renny mutters, shaking his head. "Let's wait and see if he gets Trade out, and go from there. If he wants us to owe him, something shady must be going on, and there's definitely shit he's not telling us."

"If the Destined Killers MC is involved, you know shit is going to get messy," Temper adds, standing up. "I'm going to get back to the clubhouse. Saint has Tory there, and I'm going to go and hang out with her."

"Who is Tory?" I ask.

"Saint's daughter," Renny explains, laughing at my surprised reaction.

"I had no idea that Saint has a kid… Skylar?"

"Skylar's not her biological mother," he says, explaining that Saint had Tory before he and Skylar got together.

"That makes more sense." I can't imagine Skylar having a daughter and not even mentioning it to me. Moms love to talk about their kids.

My phone rings and I stare at it when I see my dad's name. I know instantly that this isn't going to be a pleasant phone call, but curiosity has me answering anyway. "Hello?"

"Please tell me what your long-term plan is with this biker?" he asks, and I can just imagine him sitting in his office on his big chair.

"Dad," I start, taking a deep breath. "My life doesn't affect yours. No one will connect us. I'm sure the person who saw me on the bike was one of your spies, am I right? It wasn't just someone random. No one even knows who I am. The media only knows your new family."

"I don't have a new and an old family, Isabella, I just have a family," he states with such conviction that, if I hadn't experienced being left behind by him myself, I probably would have believed him. "You are all my children and I love you all the same. I'd love it even more if you and Ariel spent more time with your baby sisters."

"Don't pretend we are welcome there, Dad. Your wife has been nothing but rude to us and made sure we knew our place from the very beginning. Either you didn't care or you allowed it anyway, which is the real reason this family isn't close. Never mind how you treated my mother, who was a good woman."

"How many times are we going to have this same argument?" he asks. "And it has nothing to do with the fact that you are now dating a criminal. What happened to my smart little girl? I don't even know who you are anymore."

This comment hurts and angers me at the same time. He hasn't known me in years, and that's because of his decisions and his actions.

"We're probably going to have this same argument forever," I tell him, gritting my teeth. "Maybe I chose a biker because I have daddy issues that you caused. Don't worry about what I'm doing, it's not going to affect your latest campaign, I can assure you of that."

"Isabella—"

"I really appreciate you helping Trade," I continue, my nails digging into my palm. "So thank you for that, Dad. But if you've just called me to lecture me and tell me everything I'm doing wrong with my life, I'd rather not hear it." I pause and then add, "And by the way, if you love us all the same, how come you haven't even seen or asked about your granddaughter? Surely that should mean something to you?"

"She was born out of wedlock—"

"You cheated on your wife," I remind him. His hands are far from clean from his own judgment. "You can't just choose how you sin and decide that it's okay, but judge everyone else for their life choices. It doesn't work that way."

He takes a loud breath, like he's trying to calm himself. "At the end of the day, I'm still your father, whether you like it or not, and I'm never going to accept you being with this biker. You think I'm going to walk you down the aisle? Be there when you start a family? Leave you anything in my will? Because I won't if I don't agree with the way you're living your life."

"As if you're leaving us anything anyway, that wife of yours will make sure of that," I tell him, rolling my eyes. There's no way she's going to let him give us anything in his will; it will all go to her and her children. "I don't want any money from you, Dad. The one thing I wanted you've already destroyed, which is my childhood."

I hang up, feeling worse after my rant instead of better.

There are some people who just bring out the worst in you, and those are the people you need to avoid.

Even if they are your own flesh and blood.

Chapter Twenty-Four

About a week later I find Ariel staring at the security screen, Shadow barking like mad at the front door. "Izzy, there's a really hot guy at the front door. Who the hell is he?" she whisper-yells, pointing.

I close my laptop to give this my full attention. "I don't know, I've never seen him before."

The man at our front door is tall and tattooed, with dark features and a man bun tied on top, but underneath he has it all shaved off.

"What do we do?" she asks, throwing her hands up in the air. "Who knew living with you would be so social? You used to be a hermit."

"Come on, let's go and see who it is." Surely someone that meant us harm wouldn't just knock on the door? Although I've seen burglars on television use this technique to gain entry and then push right in with force.

"Yes?" I call out to the man.

"Hey, Izzy? I'm a friend of Renny's," he says.

I pick up my phone and call Renny.

"Hello, beautiful, I was just thinking about you."

"Do you know some brunette young guy with a man bun?" I ask him. "Because he's here and name dropping so we'll open the door."

"What? Oh, that's Trade. He wanted to say thank you, although I told the bastard to wait until I got home. I'm on my way now."

Trade? I hang up on Renny and open the door. "Hey," I tell him. "Sorry, just had to check who you are. You know, stranger danger, and all of that."

He smiles widely, flashing white teeth. I tell Shadow to stop his barking, and he does, instantly.

I don't know why but I pictured Trade as being… well…an old man. He has kids and got out of the life, so I was assuming he was older than Temper, maybe in his forties or something, but the man in front of us looks young, maybe late twenties, and doesn't look like a dad at all.

Ariel has gone oddly quiet next to me, and I know that Trade is just her type.

"No problem. Renny told me to wait for him, but I was bored and I wanted to say thank you to you both." He looks over at Ariel, and just stares for a few seconds.

I glance between them both, watching as they both visibly check each other out.

"Come on in. Renny said he's on his way. Ignore Shadow, he'll stare you down but won't bite you." Unless I tell him to.

Trade steps inside and glances around. I lead him to the kitchen, and offer him a drink. "I'd love a coffee," he replies, so I get to making us all one.

"You don't need to thank us, we didn't really do anything," I tell him. "The MC did all the hard work. I just made a phone call."

"Still, I appreciate it," he says, looking us both in the eye. "Without your dad using his contacts, who knows when I would have gotten out, and who knows if they would have given me my kids back, so thank you."

"How many kids do you have?" Ariel asks him, suddenly having found her voice.

"Three," he replies, smiling at the thought of them. "Two girls and a boy."

"Nice. They must keep you busy," she says, leaning forward on the counter. I bet she's wishing she was wearing something other than her unicorn silk pajamas, with her hair in a messy bun on top of her head. She still looks beautiful, though.

"They do. I'm a full-time dad and I work full time, so my life is pretty hectic," he replies, the two of them now having a private conversation between them as if I'm not even there anymore.

"What do you do for work?" she asks, conducting a full interview.

"I work in construction," he says, brown eyes pinned on her. "I own my own company, actually. So I can be flexible when I need to, but it also requires a lot of my time and energy. So it's basically like having four kids."

They both laugh, while I'm standing here wide-eyed, adding sugar into their mugs.

Shadow runs to the front door, letting me know that Renny is indeed here. He storms in, scowl etched onto his handsome face, dressed in all black. "I told you to wait for me."

"I was bored," Trade muses, standing back and scrubbing his hand down his freshly shaven face. "I've been at the clubhouse all day, sitting around, waiting for the call that I can go and pick up my kids. I needed a distraction."

"My woman's house isn't a place you or any other man

gets to go to for a distraction," Renny seethes, staring him down. I don't think I've ever seen him this angry before.

He comes to my side and kisses my temple. "I'm sorry you both had a random fresh-out-of-jail biker showing up at your doorstep, especially when we've just told you to be more careful."

"It's okay," I assure him, wrapping my arms around him and resting my cheek against his chest. "And before you lecture me on leaving the door unlocked, you said you were right around the corner."

He purses his lips, but chooses his battles and lets it go, too busy directing his anger at Trade, who is currently making love heart emoji eyes at my sister.

"Would you like a coffee, babe?" I ask Renny, distracting him.

I can see why he's annoyed at Trade, especially since we're all kind of waiting for the shoe to drop at any moment, but the man did just get out of prison, and like he said, is waiting for his kids to return to him. It's nice that he wanted to thank us, not that I needed to hear it because I didn't actually do much, but I appreciate the sentiment.

We all sit on the couch. I put out some snacks, and Renny and I watch Trade and Ariel hitting it off. Mila starts to cry, so I get up before Ariel can, and bring her back to the group.

Trade looks at her with wide brown eyes. "Renny?"

"Not mine," Renny replies, smirking.

Trade then eyes me, but I also shake my head and nod at Ariel.

"Mila is my daughter," she says, smiling as I hand her to her.

Realization hits him. He doesn't look disappointed or

turned off, just really surprised. "You don't look like you have a newborn child."

"Told you," I tell her.

"Well, thank you," she replies, ducking her head and giving her attention to her child. "She is an unexpected surprise, but now that she's here I can't imagine my life without her."

"I thought you were going to be an old man," I admit to Trade after a little while.

He barks out a laugh. "Why is that?"

"Temper said that you walked away from club life for your kids," I explain with a shrug. "So I thought you'd spent years with the club or something. I don't know, I just thought you were in your forties or something, older than Temper."

"I started having kids young," he says, amusement in his gaze. "I was seventeen when I had my first, so yeah, I guess I can see why you thought that. But nope, I'm the younger and better-looking brother in the family."

Ariel and I share a look, because we make similar jokes about each other all the time. I guess no matter where you live and how you grow up, one thing doesn't change, and that is that siblings are always going to give each other shit.

"And the modest one, clearly," Ariel adds, arching her brow. "How did you fit into this house with a head that big?"

I snuggle into Renny and let them have their banter. "You smell nice," I tell him, staring up at him beneath my lashes. "Were you at the bike shop?"

"Yeah, been there all morning. I'm going to hire someone else, someone who knows their shit, because the place is taking off," he says, eyes alight with excitement.

"You looking for a new job, Trade? All legitimate, nothing shady."

"You assuming that I know my shit?" Trade fires back, grinning wolfishly. "I've been doing nothing but building houses for a long time now. I haven't even gone for a ride in months."

"You forget who you're talking to? I know you, brother, and I know how fuckin' good your bike looks," Renny replies, lip twitching. "Whether you've had the time to ride it or not. She's in mint condition."

Shadow runs to the door, barking, and my eyes dart to the screen. "Who else is joining us today?" People dropping over unexpectedly used to give me anxiety, but now I feel like I'm just rolling with the punches. I like to be a good host, though, and making sure everyone is fed and watered has always been a priority of mine.

Temper stands at the door. "I'll let him in," Renny says, standing up.

"Is our house the new clubhouse?" Ariel asks, laughing to herself.

She shouldn't be complaining, though, because if Trade hadn't invited himself over here, she never would have met him, because she's never stepped through those clubhouse doors.

"What the fuck are you doing here?" Temper asks his baby brother as he enters the room. "I've been looking for you."

Trade sighs, leans back and lifts his feet up on the coffee table. "I came to visit with our lovely neighbors here. What did you want me for?" He starts to pat Shadow, who just sits there, loving the attention.

"We can go pick up the kids now," Temper says, sighing in relief. "I just got the call. Come on, let's go."

"Really?" Trade asks, jumping to his feet. "We can get them, just like that?"

Temper nods. "Yes, just like that. A deal is a deal, and the mayor came through with his end. Next month we need to come through with ours."

The two of them leave, and I feel so happy for Trade.

"So," I start, grinning at my sister. "What the hell was that?"

"What the hell was what?" she asks, kissing Mila on the forehead.

"You and Trade were eye fucking each other from the second he stepped inside," I blurt out, smile so wide my cheeks start to hurt. "Mrs. I Don't Want A Man totally wanted that man."

"He was nice to look at that's all," she replies, scowling. "I'm allowed to admire a man—that doesn't mean I want him." She turns to Renny. "And don't you dare go and say one word to him."

"My lips are sealed," Renny promises, amusement radiating from him. He rests his arm behind me and turns to me. "Do you want to come back to the clubhouse with me? I'm going to work out, and then we can go out for dinner?"

"You two eye fuck each other all the time," Ariel adds, glancing between us. "Like right now… But when I do it once…"

Renny stands and lifts me up in his arms. "Yeah, and look where we are now."

"I'm not going to marry him, that's for sure," she grumbles, standing up and heading to her room.

Hand in hand, we walk outside to his car.

He sits me on the hood of his car and kisses me, leaning me backward with a hand on my nape.

God, I love this man.

Chapter Twenty-Five

"I don't know how we're supposed to just sit here," I tell Skylar, pacing up and down the clubhouse kitchen. "What if something goes wrong?"

"I know exactly what you mean, but in this case there's nothing much we can do. If we were there we'd just be a distraction to them, and they need to concentrate on doing their job," she replies, tapping long red fingernails on the table. "Trust me, I hate it as much as you do."

The men left an hour ago when my dad called in the favor the MC owes him, which ended up being them doing security for some political event. Considering he will also have his own personal security there, it doesn't sound like it will be too much of a risk, which makes it a bit fishy. There's more going on that I don't know about. It's also highly likely that Renny left some information out when briefing me on what was going down, even though Temper admitted that there might be some added issues with a rival MC of theirs.

"When did life get so complicated?" I ask myself, sighing. I never thought I'd have to be worrying about anyone's enemies, never mind a motorcycle club's, and I never thought I'd have to worry about whether or not my man will come home.

Most of all, I never thought my dad would be involved in the same situation as all of this.

"When you accepted a ride on Renny's bike when your car fake broke down?" Skylar reminds me.

"Ahh yes. That's right." How can I forget?

Skylar studies me, a thoughtful look on her expression. "Come on, we can't just sit here and do nothing."

"Where are we going?" I ask her, following her out to her car.

"To the event."

"What about that speech you just gave me?" I ask, frowning. I don't want to be a distraction or make things harder for them in any way. I'm so out of my element right now. At the same time I'm glad that she has a plan, because sitting there and waiting is killing me.

"We won't just rock up there, we can hide and just see what the hell is going on…" She trails off when we see Crow and Chains sitting on her car.

Crow grins, crossing his arms over his chest, an amused glint in his blue eyes. "Saint told us you might try this, Skylar."

"What did he tell you? That we'd get hungry and head out to grab some food?" she lies, acting casual and relaxed. "We will be back soon."

"We've been told not to let either of you go anywhere unless we accompany you," Chains adds, seemingly unimpressed with his babysitting gig. "So if you want to get food, then we'll all go."

Shit. Saint really knows his woman, and I know how angry Skylar must be right now—he essentially left these men here to make sure she does as he had instructed.

Crow brings those blue eyes to me. "Saint said you'd corrupt Izzy."

Yeah, Saint really does know his old lady.

I throw my hands in the air. "We're going to get some food. Now if you're all coming, then come. I'm hungry."

We all get into the car, Skylar and I grabbing the front seats before they can, so the two of them are stuck in the back and unhappy about it, but too bad.

No one has a plan here, but as we drive away from the clubhouse, I'm wondering if all we're going to be able to get is some food.

"So what are we eating?" Crow asks, sticking his head in between our seats. "I heard about this new fried chicken place that just opened."

Skylar and I look at each other, having a silent conversation.

She asks me if I have a plan.

I tell her no, I don't, and that we're fucked.

She winces.

I tell her we need to get as close to the event as we can without it being obvious we're going in that direction.

"I don't know, I kind of feel like dumplings," she says, shrugging. "What do you think, Izzy?"

"Dumplings and a cocktail sound amazing right now," I agree. "Do you like Asian food, Crow?"

"Sure, why not?" he replies, sounding a little suspicious. "It might be better if we stay a little closer to home, though, don't you think?"

"Don't try to bullshit us," Chains states from the backseat. He has this growl in his tone that's kind of scary, but kind of sexy at the same time. "Tell me what you're up to."

"What if the men are in trouble?" Skylar asks them, giving up on the pretense. "I'm not going to lose any of those men, and if I can help in some way, I want to be able to. And yes, I know I'm not some badass biker, but I'm not useless. I'm smart, I'm scrappy, and I'm capable, and so is Izzy. I'm a damn EMT! Not to mention it's Izzy's dad running this whole thing, so if something goes wrong, she might be the only person who can fix it."

I never thought of it that way, but she's right, especially if my dad has plans to screw them over. He might not be father of the year, but he wouldn't want me to get hurt or to see him being shady, because he still maintains his façade of being a decent human being.

"Nothing is going to go wrong," Chains assures us. "They are staying in the back, just making sure the Killers MC doesn't decide to come to the event and start some shit."

"Which is dragging the Knights back into a war we only just got out of," Skylar replies, swallowing hard. "A war that lost me my father. So excuse me if I'm a little paranoid that something can go wrong again this time. If something happens to Saint…"

"Nothing is going to happen," Crow tells her, sighing. I can tell he's not sure what to do and has been put in a hard place between Skylar's emotional plea and what his president and patched club members have ordered him to do. "We need to be back at the clubhouse, which is where Temper wanted us to be, not driving around trying to convince you two to follow orders. The clubhouse is empty now—what if someone goes there right now?"

Skylar and I share another look, because he's right, we did leave the clubhouse empty.

"What does the clubhouse matter if one of the men die?" Skylar fires back, scowling. "The people make the clubhouse. There's nothing in there that can't be replaced."

My phone rings, and it's Renny.

Fuck.

I need to answer this.

"Hello?" I say quickly.

"Where are you?" he asks me, anger in his tone. "I got a message saying that you've left the clubhouse."

Damn, one of them snitched, and my bet is on Chains.

"We're fine," I assure him. "We're just worried about all of you. What's going on there? Is everything okay?"

"Get back home now," Renny growls. "Just listen to me, Izzy. You and Skylar get home and stay there."

"No, tell Izzy to get here. We need her, maybe she can fix this," I hear Saint call out in the background.

"What does he mean? What can I fix?" I ask Renny.

"Nothing," Renny snarls. "Just listen to me and get home. There is nothing you can do."

"Okay," I whisper, staring down at the phone as he hangs up. "We have to go back… I think."

Something has gone wrong, I can feel it in my bones, and I just hope that none of the men are hurt—or worse.

"What do you mean, you think?" Skylar asks, taking deep breaths, and I can tell she's trying to stop herself from freaking out and panicking. "What did he say?"

"Renny told me to get back to the clubhouse, but I heard Saint in the background, and he said that maybe I can fix…whatever is going on there," I explain, closing my eyes and resting my head back. "I don't know, what do we do?"

I love Renny, and I know he wants to protect me, but if I can do something to help, I'm going to.

"Saint wants you to go?" she asks, frowning.

"Yeah, and I think we should go," I declare, turning to face the men in the backseat. "Something has happened, and we need to go. I don't give a shit what either of you have to say."

"Fuck," Chains grits out, looking at his friend. "We're screwed if we do, and screwed if we don't. If we let them go and get hurt, they'll have our fuckin' heads, and if we kidnap them and drag them back to the clubhouse, they're going to make our lives hell."

"Fuck it, let's just go, they might need us," Crow agrees, nodding. "Let's do it."

He pulls out a gun from his jeans, which has my eyes boggling. "Fucking hell."

What am I getting myself into right now?

My mind flashes back to the shootout I witnessed a few weeks back, and little Billy crying next to me.

"It will be fine," Skylar assures me, reaching over and touching my shoulder. "We're all in this together."

And I guess that is the one part that makes you want to fight for this, because these people will always have my back, and I want to give them the same loyalty in return.

Skylar steps on the gas, and I hold on to the seat belt, wondering what the hell we're about to walk into.

And if we're all going to make it out.

Chapter Twenty-Six

There's a lot more people at the event than I thought there was going to be. It seems like the whole city has come to hear the mayor speak and to meet the guests he has invited. Skylar parks the car, and we all get out and slip into the busy crowd.

"What now?" I ask her, glancing around to find Renny. "I can't see any of them."

My dad is standing in front of a microphone, speaking about all of the ideas he has to make the city a better place. He has his security behind him, but none of them are the Knights.

"You stay here," I tell Skylar, Chains and Crow, pushing through the crowd, ignoring Skylar calling my name, trying to stop me. I'm the only one safe here, because Dad won't hurt me.

I stand right in front, where he can see me if he looks down, and search for any of the Knights, but come up short. I know when he lays eyes on me, because he stumbles in his proposal, then clears his throat and continues.

I look him in the eye, my expression blank. If anything has happened to Renny, I will never forgive him, because I know he had a hand in whatever has transpired today.

After the speech is over and someone takes over the

microphone, my dad takes a seat, and I decide to send Renny a text message. I'm here. Tell me what has happened.

I know how angry he's going to be, but I can deal with that later. Right now I just need to get everyone out of here alive, well and hopefully without a target on their backs. I don't see any other bikers around, unless the Killers are here incognito.

Renny doesn't reply, the first sign that the plan has gone south.

It's then that I see them, to the right of the building, standing in front of a police car. Temper is in handcuffs and is being held on the hood, facedown with two officers pinning him.

I rush over to my dad as he walks offstage. "What is going on? Why is Temper being arrested? Did you plan this?"

"No, I did not," he assures me, fixing his suit jacket and glancing around to make sure no one can hear our conversation. He pulls me to the side, farther away from anyone else. "He had a gun on him, the cops showed up. There's nothing much I can do, Isabella."

"You asked them to be here to help you," I tell him, anger making me wild. "You set this up! Didn't you? What do you get out of this?"

My father looks strained, and much older than I last saw him, the lines in his forehead more prominent, the gray hair around his face more visible. "It's not me calling the shots with this, okay?"

"That doesn't make it okay," I reply, clenching my teeth. "Dad, Temper is a good man and he doesn't deserve this. They came here to help you and to stick to their side of the deal. It's up to you to make sure they don't get arrested and go to prison over them keeping their word! Please, for me."

He studies me, scanning my eyes, just like his. "Fuck."

He walks over to where the cops are now placing Temper in the back of the police car, and says something to the officer, who looks surprised but nods.

They then let Temper free, uncuffing him.

Just like that.

It's a pretty terrifying concept, really, the fact that if you don't know someone, you're fucked, but if you do you're able to get out of any situation you manage to get yourself into. What a messed-up world we live in.

I rush over to Temper, grabbing onto his arm. "Where is Renny and the rest of the guys?"

"They went after the Killers MC," he admits, stretching his neck from side to side and cursing. "What the hell are you doing here?"

"I'm here with Skylar and we dragged your prospects into it," I say quickly, leading him in the direction of her car. "You can yell at us later. We just need to get you out of here, and we need to make sure everyone else is safe."

When he says they went after the Killers, I don't picture the best outcome. I might have been able to help in this situation because of my dad, but I don't think there's much I can do to stop two motorcycle clubs trying to kill each other.

Skylar is waiting at the car, looking worried as hell, and confusion takes over when she sees me with Temper and Temper alone.

"Rest of them went after the Killers," I explain, hoping it makes any sense. "Temper was about to get arrested."

"Go back to the clubhouse," he demands. "I'll meet you there on my bike."

We nod, and this time, do as we've been told.

I just hope that Renny is okay.

"No one is answering their phones, Temper included," Skylar says to us, pacing. "It's been over half an hour, he shouldn't have been this far behind us. He's gone after them! He made us go home, and then he went to help them."

"Makes sense." Crow nods from where he's sitting on the kitchen counter. "I'd have done something similar. He won't just sit around while his men are at war."

"We're back in the exact same spot we were in." I groan, covering my face with my hands. "This is a lot of stress and anxiety."

We hear the rumble of motorcycles and all rush to the front to open the gate as they all pull in. Renny, Temper, Saint, Dee, Trade…they're all there, along with a few faces I don't know.

Once the bikes are all parked I run to Renny and jump into his arms, kissing his face as soon as his helmet comes off.

"Thank fuck you're okay," I say as he squeezes me tightly, carrying me in his arms and walking back into the clubhouse, my legs wrapped around him and my face buried in his neck.

We all sit down at their big table, in a room I've never been invited into before.

"What happened today was a clusterfuck," Temper starts, sitting at the head of the table and eying us each in turn.

"What happened?" Skylar dares to ask.

"We did the security, everything was going fine. No drama. And then the Killers showed up, with their new president. At first it was obvious they had their eyes on Izzy's dad. But then they saw Temper and all hell broke loose," Saint explains.

"They tried to shoot him, but then the police were called in and Temper was arrested. They took off on their bikes so we went after them, along with the cops, who ended up arresting a few of the Killers members. With the cops there we just bailed, letting them handle the Killers. Eventually the whole event was shut down, and everyone had to leave."

"I think they were supposed to take out your dad," Temper admits. "Which is why he wanted us there, because he would have got wind of that. But then they saw me, and they didn't want to miss that chance."

So my dad didn't plan for Temper to get arrested, he just wasn't going to do anything to stop it. I don't know why they'd want him dead, other than his personal agenda doesn't work with theirs. I really don't know much about how these motorcycle clubs work, so who knows? My dad and I might not be close, but that doesn't mean that I want to see him hurt or killed.

"Are the cops going to come here now?" I ask, considering everything that happened today.

"Maybe," Temper replies. "Hopefully they're too busy with the Killers, who openly branded weapons and fired shots. I had my gun on me, but it's registered, and I didn't use it, openly or not. It was concealed at all times until they searched me."

My head suddenly hurts. They continue their meeting, breaking down everything that happened and what they think should happen next, and then finally I'm brought up.

"Skylar and Izzy, we told you to stay behind for your

own safety," Temper says, scowling. "However, if you hadn't come, Izzy, I would have been behind bars right now, because they arrest first and ask questions later. It would have been a fuckin' messy ordeal, so thank you. I know you both just wanted to help, but I'd appreciate it if we could count on you both to follow orders in the future.

"Crow and Chains," he continues, glancing at the two prospects. "I know these two are headstrong, but you let the women lead you. It all worked out this time, so I'm not going to be so harsh, but what would have happened if one of the women got killed? Could you imagine the fallout of that? If the men leave their women under your watch, they do so knowing you will do anything and everything in your power to keep them safe."

Crow nods. "It was hard, especially when we knew Saint wanted Izzy to go and Renny told her to stay. They made their decision and I wanted to be there to protect them during it."

"I couldn't let them all go alone," Chains throws in, clearly pissed off at the turn of events. "Like you said, our job was to make sure that they were safe, and we did that to our best ability."

"I know you did what you thought was right. But next time you have to do everything you can to just follow orders." Temper is not giving in on this.

Crow and Chains have enough smarts to just take the lashing and say nothing in response. Temper turns to Skylar, but addresses the group. "Georgia was there, too."

At the mention of this person named Georgia, all the men go on high alert as Temper continues. "I don't think that that is a coincidence. She's working with the Killers again, and while I don't quite know what she's up to, I know she wants to take us down."

"She was there?" Skylar asks, brow furrowing. "I thought she had let it all go and was moving on with her life."

"That woman can never let anything go—she's always up to something. I don't know what she wants this time, but we're going to find out," Temper bites out.

"Who is Georgia?" I whisper to Renny.

"Skylar's mom, who was behind getting her father killed," he says.

Her mom?

Shit. I don't know why I'm so surprised that an MC would have so much dysfunctional drama. Maybe because they preach loyalty?

I guess not everyone gets that memo, though.

I head back home to have a bath and a well-deserved glass of wine. Ariel is sitting on the couch breastfeeding Mila as I walk inside, and one look at my face and her expression turns from content to concern.

"What happened?" she asks, sitting up straighter. "You look drained."

"Well, the Knights were shot at and then gave chase to the bikers who shot at them. Then Temper got arrested and I had to ask Dad to tell them he was part of his security team to let him go," I start, sitting down next to her and lifting my feet up. "And apparently Dad is on the Killers MC's shit list because of something or another and they want him to disappear."

She opens her mouth, then closes it, brow furrowing in thought. "I've literally been sitting here with Mila, cleaning the house and cooking us dinner, and this is what has been going on in the meantime? Jesus Christ."

"Where's Shadow?" I ask, realizing that he hasn't come to greet me.

"He's outside," she says, lifting Mila up to burp her. "And I can't believe Dad actually helped Temper."

"To be honest I think he realized he needs the Knights. They're the only ones who can stand up to the Killers, or at least the only ones who have done so in the past," I admit, thinking over everything that I have learned from today. "I don't know, Ariel. There has to be a way out of all this bullshit without someone getting hurt. Skylar's dad, Hammer, died the last time they faced off with the Killers. Now they both have new presidents but don't want to let go of what happened."

"If someone killed someone that you loved, could you let it go, or would you forever want revenge, just waiting for the right moment?" she asks, kissing the top of Mila's head.

If anyone hurt her or Mila, I wish that I could say I would be strong enough to forgive and move on, but I don't know if I could. I don't think you ever know until you are in that situation.

"These men are a brotherhood, Izzy, and now it looks like you're involved in all of this. Are you sure you can handle it? Nothing bad has happened yet, but it almost did today. And it most likely will."

She's right. And I knew it from the start. I didn't go into this blind.

But now? I'm in way too deep to get out.

I'm in love with a Knight, and this is what comes with it.

For better or for worse.

Chapter Twenty-Seven

"Hello," I say to the lady at the door. She's holding flyers in her hand, just like the one she gave Ariel. "You still haven't found your dog?"

"No," she says, sighing with sadness, her green eyes teary. She's petite and wearing a headscarf over her hair. "I've looked everywhere. I was hoping someone might have seen him, but I'm afraid I'm having no luck."

"I'm sorry to hear that. I've been keeping an eye out," I promise. "Do you live around here?"

"A few blocks over," she admits, pointing to the right, away from the clubhouse and toward the city. "Who knows how far he could have gone by now? My name is Gia, by the way."

"I'm Izzy," I say, offering her my hand. "It's nice to meet you. I kept the flyer with your number on it, so if I see or hear anything I will give you a ring."

"That would be perfect, thank you," she says, smiling sadly. "I've met some really nice people around this neighborhood, it's just a shame that this is why. I haven't gone to the MC clubhouse, though… I wonder if they have seen my dog."

"Oh, I can ask for you," I suggest. "I don't have many

other friends to ask around here, but I can ask them, at least."

"That would be great," she says, perking up. "You know them well, then?"

"Not well," I backtrack, shrugging. "But I do know them, yes. They are nice people."

She opens her mouth to ask another question, but I cut her off before she can. "I'll call you if I find anything out, all right? Good luck."

She nods, smiles and walks away. I can't help but feel terrible for her—she must really love her dog. But talking about the MC with a total stranger isn't something I'm going to engage in any further. I wish I could do more to help, but my hands are a little full right now with everything going on with the MC and my dad.

Closing the door, I puff out a breath and walk back into the kitchen, where Renny is carrying Mila while Ariel is lecturing him on what's going to happen if I get hurt in the crossfire.

"Just remember, I know where you live," she concludes, pointing her finger at him. "And stop being so cute with my daughter while I'm trying to yell at you."

"I can't help it," he says in his baby voice. "Mila is just too cute, aren't you, Mila? How do you feel about your mommy yelling at me? You don't like it either, do you?"

I shake my head at him in amusement. "The lady came back looking for her dog."

"Aw, no. I was hoping she'd have found him by now," Ariel says, stirring the pot of pasta she's making. "I haven't seen any dog around, and I've been looking."

"I know, I said the same. Don't be getting clucky over there, mister," I say to Renny, who is looking at Mila with a little too much love in his eyes. "I know she's cute, but the best thing about her is that you get to return her."

"Can men get clucky?" he asks, grinning. "She's just really cute, all right? Give me a break. Don't worry, I'm not going to ask you for a baby." He pauses, and then adds, "For at least the next three years."

My mouth gapes.

I can't believe he just said that.

"What? We were already married, isn't that the natural progression of things?" he asks, chuckling at my unamused expression.

"No, getting remarried would be next." Ariel smirks, glancing between the two of us. "In due time, of course."

"I have a plan, don't worry," he replies, winking at me. I don't know what plan he's talking about, but if things are going how they are going and we do remain a couple long-term, I'd like a proper proposal and wedding, because that one definitely didn't count.

"Are you going to share this plan with me?" I ask, arching my brow.

I've always said that I'd only get married once, but for the same man, I'll make an exception.

He just laughs and continues to fuss over Mila. Ariel throws me an amused look, and I know she's thinking the same thing as me.

Renny wants to remarry and have kids with me one day.

I'd say that I don't know how to feel about that, but the smile on my lips speaks for itself.

When Dad calls and asks if he can come over for a chat, I hesitantly agree. One, he's never been to my house before. I've always gone to his mansion instead. But we definitely do have things to discuss, and it would be nice for him to finally meet Mila. Not to mention that if I'm going to see him, I'd rather do it without his wife present, because no one needs that in their lives.

I hate that we tidy the house and cook a meal knowing he's coming, and I hate that we get dressed and look decent, presenting this picture of us having our lives all sorted and put together.

I guess no matter how far you come, some things will never change, and secretly wanting parental approval is one of them. Or maybe we just want to show him how much we have succeeded in life without him. Without his time, without his money and without his support, we have banded together as our own mini family, and we are thriving.

And we want to show him we don't need him.

He shows up straight from work, in a navy blue suit jacket with a white shirt, his dark hair unkempt and messy, like he's been running his hands through it in frustration.

"Hey," I say to him, opening the door and letting him inside. I can hear Shadow barking from outside, but ignore him and offer my dad a seat. "Do you want a coffee or tea or something?"

So formal. Any other parent would probably just walk in and make themselves at home, I imagine, but with him it's almost like having a stranger enter your premises.

"Coffee would be nice," he replies, sitting down and looking around.

Ariel walks out with Mila in her arms. "Hey, Dad."

"Hey, Ariel. So this is Mila," he murmurs, standing up and walking over to them. He holds out his arms, and although Ariel hesitates, she ends up letting him hold her. "She looks just like you did as a baby."

"I know. I did a comparison photo and we look pretty much exactly the same. Same green eyes, dark hair and lips. I think she only got her nose from her dad."

Dad sits down and just watches Mila. "I'm sorry I'm only meeting her now."

He doesn't say anything else, no explanations, no *I'll come around more*, just a sorry. Ariel doesn't say anything in return, and I don't know how she's expected to answer.

"What did you want to discuss?" I ask, placing his mug on the coffee table and sitting down.

"We can start with what happened the other day," he says, eying me. "You were reckless. You knew something could have gone wrong that day, but you showed up anyway."

"And if I didn't you would have let Temper get arrested, and they would have found some bullshit reason to keep him locked up," I say.

Or legit reason, but that doesn't sound too good for my argument.

"At the end of the day, the Knights were there to protect you, and you need them to handle the Killers, who you've apparently pissed off," I continue, using what I know will work on him.

"We kicked them out of their clubhouse and knocked it down," Dad admits, handing Mila back to Ariel and wincing. "And yeah, I made the final decision on that. I was hoping they'd leave town, because they're all a bunch of criminals and make the city look bad."

My jaw drops. "Yeah, that would do it."

Imagine how angry everyone would be if the council did that to the Knights?

"How did you kick them out? Isn't it their property?" I ask, wondering how the hell that could have been legal.

"We have our ways," he replies, sniffing.

"So you bribed someone," I guess out loud, shaking my head. "You guys are basically like an MC without the bikes—you still do shady things, you still think the law doesn't apply to you, and you have no problems running over other people to get what you want."

"And you have no problem dating one of them," Dad reminds me, scowling. "So don't throw stones at glass houses, Isabella. You can't judge my character, because look at who you have surrounded yourself with."

"Renny is a good man," I defend, lifting my chin. "And if that's why you're here, you're wasting your time because I'm not walking away from him."

"I'm here because I'm worried about you both. You have a baby to worry about now, so it's not exactly the time to be getting mixed in all of this. And if the Killers are targeting me, you don't think they're going to try and go after my family? Especially considering one of them has ties to their other enemies."

The man has a point.

"Well, your other family is safe behind those massive gates back at the mansion," Ariel adds, shrugging. "Don't worry about us. Most people don't know about your connection to us, and we have the MC for protection."

"You're both alone here, with a newborn," he states, tone full of disbelief. "Yeah, I'm sure the MC will protect you, but they aren't exactly here twenty-four seven, are they?"

"We will manage," Ariel says, no emotion on her face.

"Don't worry about us, Dad, worry about yourself, because you might have been shot dead the other day."

"I know, and the cops are on them. The Knights being there has drawn most of them out. A few of them have been arrested, which is why things might be quiet for a while, but they couldn't place all of them at the event," he admits, rubbing the back of his neck. "And I let them know the Knights were there to help me, so the cops will be leaving you all alone."

"Thank you," I say, meaning it.

"You're welcome," he replies, taking a sip of his coffee, then glancing into the mug. "It tastes just like how your mom used to make it."

We all go silent.

Mom taught me how to make coffee, so of course it tastes just like hers, but as usual when he mentions her we all freeze up.

"I do miss her," he continues, either not picking up on the sudden frost in the air or just not caring. "Regardless of what you two think, I did love your mom, and I always will. She was a great woman."

"We know," I finally say. "She never said a bad thing about you, even after all that you did to her. She was graceful right up until the end. I don't know if I could have had that strength."

In fact, I know I couldn't, because I'm holding on to her grudge for her.

"You do have her strength," he finally says, standing up and looking between the two of us. "If you need a safe place to stay, call me. I can put you in one of my houses, or you are always welcome to come and stay at mine."

"Okay, thanks," I say.

"You stay safe, too," Ariel says before he leaves the room.

"Don't worry, before I'm through all of the Killers MC will be behind bars," he calls out. I hear the door close behind him.

I can't help but think the real reason he wanted the Knights there was to draw them out, as he said, so he could get rid of them once and for all. I wouldn't put it past him—he's always one step ahead, using whoever he needs to get what he wants.

"Well, Mila, that was your grandfather," Ariel says to her daughter.

"We should have taken a photo or something," I muse. "For when Mila is older. But I guess she can always just search him online."

"I'm surprised he didn't lecture me on Merve. He always did hate him."

"I guess I'm the bigger disappointment to him right now so I'm taking all the heat for you," I grumble, reaching out to let Mila hold my thumb in her hand.

"I appreciate that," Ariel says, laughing softly. "How did we turn out so normal?"

"Did we turn out normal?"

She thinks about it. "At least we aren't assholes."

"Fair."

"And at least we have each other," she says, reaching out to squeeze my face. "We're a two-woman army."

I smile.

And she's right, we are.

Chapter Twenty-Eight

I can tell that something isn't right the second I step onto my property. Shadow, who is on the lead with me, starts barking, but it isn't his usual bark. There's an aggression and a panic in there that I haven't heard before, and it sets me right on edge.

Rushing to the front door, which is unlocked, I step inside the house and let Shadow off his lead. He runs around the house, sniffing and barking.

"Ariel?" I yell, rushing to her room, but she's not there. And neither is Mila.

I call her phone, but she doesn't pick up, so I contact Renny straight away. "Hey, babe," he says, and I can hear the smile in his tone.

"Can you come here now?" I ask, rushing the words out. "Ariel and Mila aren't here, and the door was unlocked..."

"I'm on my way," he says, then hangs up.

I try to call her a few more times, but she doesn't pick up. There's nothing missing, no sign of struggle in the house, and her car is still here, so I know she hasn't gone anywhere. I asked her if she wanted to come for a walk with me and Shadow, but she declined because Mila was asleep, so it makes no sense for her to go for a walk either.

Renny rushes into the house and I give him a quick rundown. He goes to the security monitor and checks the footage. I don't know why I didn't think of that, probably because I was freaking out and not thinking straight.

"Here," he says, pointing to the footage. A man comes to the front door, and Ariel opens it. He then pushes inside and pulls out a knife, demanding that she and Mila leave with him or he's going to kill the baby.

My heart in my throat, tears drip down my cheeks. I've never been this scared in my life. If something happens to either of them… "What if he's hurt them already?"

"Don't think like that. We're going to save them, all right?" he assures me, cupping my face with his hands. "I need you to tell me all the information you know about the man, okay?"

"It's Merve, Mila's father," I say.

"Write his full name, address, anything you know about him down for me, while I ring Temper," he commands, taking control of the situation.

I pull out the pad of paper and pen from my bag and write down any information I know about Merve that might help them locate him. I hear Renny calling in Temper, telling him we need them all, and for them to all come to my house because it's an emergency.

I can't believe Merve did this. We always knew he was a lowlife, but I didn't think he'd actually harm his own child, or threaten to. I don't know how he found us, but he must be angry that we moved away without telling him. He never tried to contact Ariel, though. Like she said, her phone number was the same, and he never bothered reaching out or asking when he could see Mila next.

This whole time I've been worried about what the Killers might do next, I didn't even peg Merve as a threat, and now he's blindsided us by pulling this bullshit.

The rumble of motorcycles comforts me. It's not long before all the men jump off their bikes and pile into my house.

"What happened?" asks Trade, brown eyes filled with worry. "Tell me everything."

Renny gives everyone a quick recap, shows them the footage and then hands them the paper with Merve's information on it. "From the camera footage I managed to get the license plate number off the car he was driving, so I'm going to run with that," he says.

"We'll find them," Temper assures me, touching my hair. "And we will deal with that piece of shit once and for all."

I nod and watch as they all scatter, trying to find this man before anything happens to my loved ones. "Do you need someone to run that plate?" I ask Renny. "I can call my dad."

"That might be the quickest way," he admits, kissing the top of my head. "You call him and tell him what has happened. If we can use his contacts, we'll find them a lot faster."

Dad answers on the third ring. "Hello? Isabella?"

"Merve kidnapped Ariel and Mila," I say, voice breaking. "We have the license plate number of the car he was driving. Any chance you could run it and help us find them?"

"Fucking prick," he mutters, but agrees. "Yes, of course. Text me the number. I'll get the cops on it right away."

He hangs up and I look up at Renny. "I'm going to kill him with my bare hands."

"Not if we get to him first."

Dad said the MC would bring us down, would get us hurt, but they're the ones that are helping us right now.

And I know they won't stop until Ariel and Mila are home, safe, where they belong.

And as for Merve?

He'll get what's coming to him.

"He's using a stolen car," Dad says when he calls me back. "It belongs to a woman who reported it missing a few hours ago."

At least we can add that to his "reasons he should be in prison" list, which is quickly accumulating bullet points.

"So now what?" I ask, frowning. Merve's not from here so where the hell would he go and who would he stay with?

"The cops are on it, we're going to be tracing him," Dad says. "Don't worry, they will be found."

He hangs up and I turn to Renny, who is on the phone to Trade, discussing their plan of action. Everyone has been out searching for the car, knowing he can't be too far away, and Temper has been checking all the local motels and hotels.

I'm not sure what I can do to help. I feel so useless. I know that someone has to stay here at the home base just in case, but it's really hard having to sit here and play the waiting game, hoping someone finds them.

What is Merve's plan for them? I see cases like this all the time on the news, and they never end well. Maybe he wants to scare Ariel, or maybe he wants to keep Mila and get rid of Ariel. I don't know how I'm going to cope if anything has happened to them.

I wish I had been home when this happened, although

he was probably waiting for the moment when I wasn't there, along with Shadow.

In the video he says he just wanted to see Mila because he missed her. Ariel let him in because she was trying to do the right thing and never wanted to keep Merve away from his daughter, and look where it got her. She should have never answered the door. Instead she should have called me, or Renny, or anyone, and told us that her baby daddy was there.

Renny hangs up with Trade and comes over to me. I know he's itching to get out there and look for them, but he doesn't want to leave me here alone.

"You can go and join them if you want," I tell him, brow furrowing. "The more people out looking, the better." I also need to stay here in case Dad or the cops drop by asking for more information.

He's about to reply to me when his phone rings. I see Temper's name pop up.

"Hello?" Renny says. "Yeah? Oh, fuck. Okay. What do you want to do with him? Okay. Message me the address. Bye.

"They found them, let's go," he says after he hangs up, grabbing my arm and leading me to my car. "Temper saw the car out the front of an old dingy motel about fifteen minutes from here."

I message Dad and tell them we have located them. "Do we want the cops there to arrest him?" I ask Renny.

I know they'd probably prefer to hand out their own form of punishment, but if he's arrested and put in prison, that's the best outcome we can get.

"Yeah, that's probably the safest bet," he replies, pressing on the gas, trying to get us to there in record time.

"Are they safe?" I ask, wringing my hands in worry.

"Is Temper waiting outside or did he break into their room?"

"He was speaking with the front desk and asking them which room," he explains. "So I imagine he's breaking into the room right now."

"He found them pretty fast," I say, relief filling me. I wasn't sure if we were going to find them, because potentially Merve could have just kept driving over to the next state, and then our chances of finding them would have been low.

"I wish we could say that this is our first kidnapping rodeo, but it's not," Renny admits, reaching over and touching my hand. "We all know what we're doing and we work as a team."

"I can see that," I say. "You found them before the police even did."

And I've never been more grateful.

When we pull up to the motel I see Temper's bike there, and point to it. Renny parks next to him and we get out. A quick check of Renny's phone gives us the room number, and we run there, finding the room door wide open.

Stepping inside, I want to cry in relief when I see Ariel, sitting on the bed, mostly unharmed, Mila in her arms. Rushing to them, I wrap my arms around my sister, taking deep breaths, stroking her hair and thanking God that she is okay.

If anything had happened to her...

Ariel has a red mark on her face, like she's been backhanded, but she's alive and well, and that's all that matters right now. "Is Mila okay?" I ask her.

She nods, tears falling. "She's fine."

"Good," I whisper, glancing down at my niece. I have so much love for these two, and words can't express how broken I'd have been if we hadn't been able to locate them before Merve did something stupid like hurt them.

I turn to find him sitting with his back against the wall, Temper in front of him with a knife in his hand. It must have been the knife Merve used to get Ariel and Mila into the car.

"You're such a piece of shit," I say to him, hands curling into fists. "I hope you rot in prison for the rest of your life."

"And if you don't, we'll be right here waiting for you," Renny adds, smirking. "You fucked with the wrong sisters."

"She should go to prison for taking my daughter away from me!" he snarls, staring daggers at Ariel. "She moved away without even telling me! Who does that? It's her who should be punished. You will all get what's coming for you, don't you worry about that."

He's completely lost it. He starts laughing, and the sound sets me on edge.

"You didn't show up to any of the lawyer meetings," I remind him, shaking my head. "You didn't answer your phone, and you've only seen your daughter twice for like twenty minutes each, so stop pretending that you're father of the year, because you're not. This just proves Mila is so much better off without you."

It never ceases to amaze me how people try to justify their actions, or never take any responsibility. It's always someone else's fault, never their own, even though he kidnapped them and had who knows what planned.

I don't know if he's on drugs, or maybe just needs some mental health assistance, but something is not right with him, and I know he hasn't always been this way. The Merve I met was charming, witty and intelligent, so I'm unsure how he became the person he is right now, but I hope he gets some help.

The cops arrive, and with my dad, luckily, because I'm sure otherwise they would have also arrested Temper for standing there with a weapon in his hands.

Dad hugs Ariel and kisses her temple, and it's the most affection I've seen him give her in years. Afterward, he comes over to me and does the same. "I thought I'd lost them both," he admits. "When I hadn't even got to spend any time with them." He turns to Renny. "Nice to see you again, Renny."

"You, too, sir," Renny replies, taking my hand in his. "Thank you for helping us."

"You don't need to thank me. I'd do anything for my family," Dad replies, smiling sadly, before leaving. He doesn't even stick around. Obviously just knowing that Ariel and Mila are okay is enough for him, or maybe he doesn't feel like he's wanted here.

I feel kind of bad for him, but at the same time I don't, because it's his choices that have led us all to this position right now, where we're family but we're not close, because he felt it was all too hard.

"Let's go home," I tell Ariel after the police finish their questioning, wrapping my arm around her. "Don't you ever scare me like that again, you hear me?"

"I'll try not to," she replies, cradling Mila against her chest and walking with me to the car. She stops and turns, as if she suddenly remembers something, and gives me Mila. She then walks back up to Temper and gives him a big hug.

"Thank you," she says. "To you and all of the Knights." She then runs back to me.

Thank you, I mouth to him before getting into the car.

I almost lost my heart today, and if that doesn't make you appreciate life more, I don't know what does.

Chapter Twenty-Nine

"How is she doing?" Renny asks, coming up from behind and wrapping his arms around me.

"She had a shower and is now in bed," I say, turning around to face him. "I think she just wants to sleep it off and pretend that it never happened."

If only it were that easy.

"I don't think I've ever been so scared in my life than I was today," I admit, burying my face against him, his familiar scent a comfort.

"I know, but it's over now and they're safe. Merve will be locked away, and we won't have to worry about him," he assures me, rubbing my back. "And when they let him out...we can worry about that then."

"She needs to get the sole custody paperwork sorted now," I say.

"I know, Trade is going to speak to our lawyer about it today, don't worry. We will take care of it all."

Pressing my palms against his chest, I glance up at him. "How did I get so lucky?"

"Well, it all started when you wore that red bathing suit to wash your car..." he teases, lifting me up on the counter and kissing me. "You know I'd do anything for you, right?"

I nod. "I think you proved that today."

Renny and the MC had my back when I needed it most, and I've never had anyone other than my mom and Ariel be like that for me. To me, blood has always been thicker than water, but the MC treats each other just like blood. Now I know that family is what you make of it, and you can choose who you want to be in your family.

"We look after our own," he murmurs, kissing me again. "I love you, Izzy, and I want you to be mine, now and forever."

Cupping his stubbled cheeks with my palms, I look into his brown eyes. "I love you, too, Renny. And I'm grateful to have you in my life."

Pressing my forehead against his, I close my eyes and just savor the moment. Right now under my roof I have all the people who are important to me, and they are all safe and healthy. That makes me extremely lucky.

"Thank you for believing in me and giving me a second chance. You won't regret it," he says, kissing me again, pulling back and looking into my eyes, and then kissing me once more.

I don't miss the heat in his gaze, but we're both going to have to wait for that.

Trade stops by with flowers, which is really fucking cute, and when I tell him that Ariel is asleep but he's welcome to wait for her, he places the bouquet on the kitchen table and leaves.

"His kids are at the clubhouse right now," Renny explains after he disappears. "I think he's going to stay for a few days before returning back to his old life."

"So he's not going to be around after that?" I ask, frowning. I know the timing is far from right, but there's definitely something there between him and Ariel, and

I didn't miss how frantic and worried he was when she went missing. There's a connection there, and it would be sad if he just went off the grid and we never saw him again.

"I'm not sure," Renny says, running his palm down his stubble. "You never know with Trade. He's always been a bit of a nomad."

"It was nice of him to bring Ariel flowers."

"Yeah, it was," Renny admits, suspicion in his tone. "I didn't think he was the flowers type."

"Were you the flowers type?" I tease, moving across the couch to sit on his lap, my arms around his neck.

"Nope. The right woman makes you the flowers type," he says, eyes widening in realization.

"Really, you're only getting this now?" I ask, smirking. "They've been eying each other since the moment that they met."

"I'm usually only paying attention to you, not who the other Knights are checking out," he mutters, then adds, "Unless they're checking you out. I definitely notice that. Like with Crow."

"He wasn't checking me out," I groan, rolling my eyes. "And you have nothing to worry about. You're the only one I want."

"I better be," he murmurs, trailing his finger across my breast, just a light touch, but it sends a shiver down my spine and makes me tighten my thighs together. "Because I'm crazy about you."

Ariel wakes up and wanders into the room, stopping when she sees us. "Don't let me interrupt you."

"You have flowers," I tell her, pointing to the table.

"From who?" she asks, bringing them to her nose and

smelling them. "They're beautiful. I can't remember the last time someone sent me flowers."

"Trade. He dropped by to see you, but you were asleep," I say, watching her reaction. She smiles like an idiot, but then puts the flowers down and heads into the kitchen to have a glass of water.

"Who knew that 'sorry you've been kidnapped' flowers are a thing?" she says without emotion. "I can't believe today even happened. I'm so glad I don't have to worry about Merve anymore."

"We all are," I say on a sigh. "We all are."

I try to bring some normalcy to my life the next day and stick to my usual routine. I do some brochures for a new company that wants to change their brand, and design a website for another. I keep an eye on Ariel to make sure that she's okay, and although a bit shaken up, she seems to be doing fine, even cracking jokes about it.

"I need to get out of the house," she declares, stepping into the living room dressed up in jeans and a tank top, Mila in a car seat. "Where can I go with a six-week-old baby? She's too young to do anything."

"You're wearing jeans? I've seen you in nothing but leggings since you gave birth," I point out.

"I know, I thought I'd change it up a little," she says, shrugging.

"I don't know where you can take a baby that young that she'd actually enjoy, but I'm sure you can go out for coffee or something. You know I can always watch her for you if you want some me time," I say, placing my laptop to the side. "You know I don't mind."

"I know, but I thought it would be nice to get her out

of the house, too," she explains. "And look, I dressed her up in one of the outfits you got her. How cute is she?"

"Adorable," I say, smiling at the little matching head-band, dress and leggings. "Red is definitely her color. Do you want me to come with you?" I don't want her to feel like I'm trying to baby her, but the ordeal did only happen yesterday, and I want her to look after herself and take it easy.

"No, I'm fine, Izzy," she assures me, picking up Mila and heading to the front door. "I'll be back soon!"

I close my laptop and glance down at Shadow. "I'm being ridiculous, aren't I? Merve is gone, what else can possibly happen?"

Shadow sighs.

"I feel the exact same way, buddy."

I decide to walk over with Shadow to the clubhouse, where I find Renny and Saint boxing each other out in the backyard. I sit down next to Skylar, who is watching them with a cocktail in her hand. "Enjoying the show?" I ask her, amused.

"You know it. You missed Crow and Chains beat the crap out of each other, it was a good fight," she says, taking a sip of her cocktail. "Would you like a drink?"

"No, I'm good, thanks. I'm meant to be working but I thought I'd drop in and see what my man is up to," I reply, wincing when Saint's fist goes just a little too close to the face I love.

"Your man. I heard you two are officially back to-gether now," she says, smiling at me. "I'm so happy for you both. I was worried there for a little while."

"So was I," I admit, looking away as Renny hits Saint hard in the stomach. "I don't know how you can watch this."

"I grew up around this kind of stuff," she says with a shrug. "It's normal life for me. It used to be a lot worse, trust me. I also have brothers, and you know boys, they fight a lot."

We couldn't have had more different upbringings. "I have no brothers," I tell her. "So this is kind of rough for me."

"Is it just you and Ariel?"

"I have two other younger half sisters, but I rarely see them," I tell her, closing my eyes as Saint gets in a shot on Renny's pretty face. "So yeah, pretty much it is just me and Ariel. Can you leave his face alone, Saint?" I call out.

Skylar laughs softly, just as Crow comes out to sit with us, sporting a black eye and a grin. "Look at you, Skylar, still sitting here with your drink, enjoying the blood and violence."

"Hey, I was sitting out here first, enjoying the sun. You guys are the ones who came out here and tried to kill each other," she says, sticking her tongue out. "You sure you don't want a drink, Izzy? I feel like an alcoholic over here."

"I'll have one," Crow says, removing his black sneakers and putting his feet up. "I think we all deserve one, it's been a long month."

Understatement of the year.

"Sorry if we got you in trouble," I say, patting him on the shoulder. "I'd like to say that we'll behave and actually listen to you next time…"

"But that would be a flat-out lie," Skylar finishes, grabbing a glass and pouring from the jug she has made. She fixes Crow a drink, even with a lemon garnish on the side, and slides it over to him. "I'm here all week."

Renny comes out and kisses me, pressing his sweaty body against mine. "I thought you were working all day."

"I am," I reply, pushing him away and laughing as he tries to kiss me more. "I just wanted to see what you were up to."

"Everything okay?" he asks, pouring himself a drink. "Do you want one?"

"No, I'm good, and yes, everything is okay. Ariel went out with Mila, and I was alone in the house, so I thought I'd bring Shadow over."

"Where is he then?" he asks, glancing around the yard.

"He went straight into your room and jumped on the bed for a nap," I admit, laughing. "And it's your fault for letting him up on there last time."

"Ariel probably needed to take control back over her life, make her feel like she's in control and independent," Renny says, pushing an errant lock of hair out of my eyes. "She's strong, and she will be fine. Don't stress. There are some things you can't save her from, she needs to figure them out for herself."

I know he's right, but that doesn't help the fact that she went through something yesterday. She could have died, and we all know that.

My sister, my best friend, my family.

And I almost lost her and her daughter.

It's a hard pill to swallow, and it's even harder to know that from now on, I'll always have to watch my back.

Chapter Thirty

Renny steps into the kitchen, freshly showered, dressed in his black leather. "Ready to go for a ride?" he asks me, leaning over to kiss the top of my head.

After all the drama and commotion, Renny wants to take me for a ride and out to eat, and just have some relaxing alone time with me, which sounds really nice. Over the last week I've really struggled with leaving the house without Ariel. My anxiety kicking in and making me want to be near them at all times, just because I never want to come home to them missing again. I know the chances of that happening again are extremely low, but I never want to be in that position again.

Renny has been slowly encouraging me to relax, because I can't live that way, he's right. I can't live in fear, because it will drain me, and I won't be able to enjoy life like I want to. Life is short enough, and I need to live in the moment.

"Yeah, I'm ready," I reply, finishing the last of my morning fuel.

We stop back at the park that will forever be known as his park, to me anyway, and Renny pulls out a little picnic I didn't even know he had packed in his leather saddlebag.

"I love this park," I say, sliding my sunglasses on to shield my eyes from the bright light. "I just imagine you playing here as a child, getting into trouble."

"The view is definitely amazing," he replies, looking at me.

After we eat, we lie down on the tartan picnic blanket, wrapped in each other's arms, whispering sweet nothings and laughing. When you're with someone and you don't need to be doing anything, you can just enjoy being next to them, touching them, I think that's when you know you've found the right person.

The person who makes you happy by just being around them.

You don't need anything else, just them.

They become your home, your comfort zone, your happy place.

Renny is all of that for me, and more, and I'm thankful for the day he rode into my life and never left.

We stop at his apartment on the way home, and the second the door is closed behind us, my back is against the wall and his lips on mine. The tension has been building between us all day, and I've been waiting for the moment I can get him alone like this, my body craving his.

"I've been looking at those red lips of yours all day, waiting for this," he says against my mouth, removing my cardigan and letting it fall to the floor. My shoes and jeans are next, leaving me in my black lace panties and a black strapless top.

He reaches for me but I step aside, arching my brow at him, then running to his bedroom, or at least trying to. He grabs me before I make it there and spins me around and kisses me more—hungry, deep kisses. He holds the back of my nape, controlling my body, then picks me up and carries me the rest of the way to his black-satin-covered bed, and all but throws me on there. He hastily removes his clothes, and I watch through heavy-lidded eyes as he returns to the bed in all his naked glory, pulling down my top and panties so we're both on an even playing field.

He flashes me a smile as he spreads my thighs and lowers his head, his pink tongue peeking out for a taste, moaning, before going down on me properly. I want to look but my head falls back and eyes close of their own accord, pleasure overtaking my system. I've never been with someone who enjoys and actually gets turned on from this act; I wasn't even sure if men like this existed. He makes more moaning noises which have me so wet, I can feel it all over my inner thighs. I can feel myself close to coming, so I try to squirm away a little, because I'm not ready for this to be over yet.

Not even close.

"Not yet," I tell him as he continues to deliciously torture my clit.

He lifts his head, wipes his mouth with the back of his hand and leans over me, pressing his hard cock against me and slowly pushing inside. I hold on to his thighs, lifting my hips up and pushing back against him. He plays with my nipples with his tongue, gently nibbling at them, shooting pleasure straight to my lower stomach.

"So beautiful," he murmurs, staring down at my body and then my face, looking me in the eye. "I'm such a lucky man."

Yes, he is, but my mouth won't seem to work right now, too lost in my head and in my body's reactions to his lovemaking.

He pulls out again and lowers his mouth back to my

pussy, and this time I can't stop the orgasm from hitting with full force, my back arching off the bed as each wave hits me. He drags it out for as long as he can, his tongue never stopping its movement until I'm limp on the bed, sated and sensitive, and only then does he slide back inside of me and continue.

Flicking my hair off my face, he presses his body against mine and kisses me. I can taste myself, but I don't care, I kiss him back, holding on to his neck and pulling him closer to me. Pushing at his chest until he rolls over, I take control, placing my hands on him and riding him. I love watching his facial expressions—the pleasure that crosses over them is my undoing every time.

Sitting back, I play with my breasts as he watches, grinding my hips on him so slowly, I know it must be driving him crazy. Proving me right, he soon moves me off him and lays me on my stomach, sliding into me from behind. He reaches underneath us and plays with my clit until I come a second time, and only then does he join me.

"Fuck," he grits out as he finishes, making growling sounds that have me wanting to jump him again.

We lie next to each other afterward, our fingers touching as we both stare up at the ceiling.

"I love you," he says.

"I know," I reply, lip twitching.

And I do.

A love like this is something that's hard to find, and although it's not perfect, it will always be enough for me.

I roll over and rest my head on his chest. Even though I'm hot and sweaty, I still want to be close to him. "It's been a while since we've been back to your sex den."

Renny chuckles. "Our sex den. I can't believe you thought this is where I brought all of my women."

"Come on, it's a valid conclusion to make," I reply, frowning. "Your own private space, where you can be as loud as you want and no one can hear you."

"You think we're shy about being loud in the clubhouse?" he asks, chuckling deeper. "We're not. No one cares. We're all men and we all have needs, and we're all adults."

"Yeah, I think you should stop talking," I tell him, rolling my eyes.

He pulls me back down next to him. "Any women I've been with in the past don't matter. The only thing that matters now is you, and trust me, I'd be an idiot to fuck this up. I'm not going to do anything to lose you, all right? It's me and you against the world."

"I know," I say. "I trust you. I wouldn't be here right now if I didn't."

We take a long, hot shower together and then head back home.

And yeah, Ariel and Mila are still there when we arrive.

Chapter Thirty-One

I wake up to voices. Throwing my robe on, I head into the kitchen, where I see Trade holding Mila while Ariel makes some breakfast.

"Good morning," I say to both, eying them in turn. Trade hasn't been here since he dropped the flowers off, and I wonder how he invited himself over this time.

"Trade dropped by on his way to work to see how I was doing," Ariel explains after I just stand there, staring at them. "Do you want some breakfast? I'm making us bacon pancakes."

"I'd love some," I say, smiling as Trade coos at Mila, similar to the way Renny acts with her. "Where are your little ones today?"

"At school," he says, glancing up at me. "My youngest just started kindergarten. It's kind of weird not having any of them at home during the day, but easier with work because I don't have to put them into daycare."

He's obviously a hardworking man, and a good father. He might be a little rough around the edges, but not more so than Temper. From what I've heard they didn't have the best childhood and found the biker lifestyle appealing at a young age.

"You should be proud of yourself," I say. "Working and kids sounds like two full-time jobs put together."

He just smiles. "Someone has to do it, hey?"

I nod, because I know what he means. It's amazing what you can do when you have no choice.

Disappearing into my bedroom, I give them some time alone and have a shower and get ready to start my day. I never thought I'd see Ariel with a biker, especially after the shit she gave me at the start for being with Renny, but as long as she's happy and safe, I will always support any decisions she makes.

By the time I make it back out there, my food is on the table but Trade has already left for work. "What was that?" I ask, eyes wide.

"What was what?" she asks, playing dumb.

"That felt like a date I was intruding on," I admit, grabbing a fork and sitting down at the table. "I felt like a third wheel and you guys haven't even spent any time alone together yet."

She purses her lips. "He's just a nice guy, checking up on me because I was kidnapped."

"Most of the men at the clubhouse are nice and care about us, but I don't see any of them dropping in with flowers to see how you are."

"Well, he's obviously the nicest," she says, shrugging. "I don't know, and don't give me any shit, because I already have no idea what I'm doing."

I nod, staying quiet for a few moments. Unable to help myself, I say, "If you two get together, you'd have gone from having no kids to having four within a few months."

If looks could kill, I'd be dead before any bacon even hit my mouth.

"You're getting a little ahead of yourself there," she

replies, sitting down with Mila in her arms. "I'm not going to rush into anything, okay? If he wants to be a friend, that would be nice, but that's about all I can take on right now."

"Friends are good," I agree.

It's also a great foundation to start a relationship on, if ever they are ready.

"Is Dad still coming over today?" she asks, changing the subject.

"Yeah, he's meant to be dropping in with Eliza and Lucy," I reply, referring to our younger half sisters. "He said he wants them to meet Mila."

She tilts her head to the side, considering. "Do you think he genuinely wants to be a part of our lives now? You know he's probably getting a lot of shit from his wife for coming here, especially with the girls."

"I know," I agree, chewing and swallowing thoughtfully. "She must hate it, and is probably making his life a living hell. She's not coming today, is she? Because I might not call Shadow off if she is."

"Nah, he wouldn't," she says, smirking. "Or more to the point, she wouldn't."

"I don't know why she hates us so much. It would be like you hating Trade's kids and not wanting him to have anything to do with them—it's stupid." I groan, rolling my eyes just thinking of her. "How can you want to have kids with someone who wasn't a good dad to the kids he already had?"

"I don't know," she says, glancing down at Mila. "I could never be with someone who didn't love my daughter. She will always come first to me."

"That's how it's meant to be," I say, finishing off my meal. "Thank you for breakfast, it was delicious." Even though she was really making it for Trade, and I just happened to stumble across it at the right time.

"You're welcome."

We both tidy up, and then I do some work until Dad arrives. I put Shadow outside so he doesn't scare the girls. I wish I didn't feel awkward around them, but I don't know them, so it doesn't feel like my sisters are coming to visit. More like distant cousins or something.

"Hello," I say to them both, smiling. "You've both gotten so big."

They both look like their mom, with light hair and eyes, both lean and very feminine looking. "I'm fourteen now," Eliza says proudly. "Only a few more years and Daddy says he will buy me a car."

"An expensive car," Lucy adds with an eye roll.

I share a look with Ariel, one that says *and this is why we don't see them often.* Their mom has raised them completely differently from how we were raised, and they are very spoiled and entitled. Still, they are family, and I'm older than them, so I try to make an effort.

"Can I get any of you something to eat or drink?" I ask, while Dad sits down and holds Mila in his arms. He even brought a gift with him this time, something Ariel thanks him for but doesn't open just yet.

"I'll have coffee," Dad says to me, looking to the girls. "Do you want something? Eliza? Lucy?"

"No thanks. Can we get something on the way home instead? I want a smoothie," Eliza says, sitting down and staring at Mila. "So this is my niece?"

"Yes," Dad says, watching me from the corner of his eye. "You are both Mila's aunties. Isn't she cute?"

The girls don't reply. And then Eliza says, "Mom said

that Ariel was stupid to have a baby when she wasn't married and that the dad tried to kill her."

My jaw drops. I knew the girls could be a little rude, but I had no idea that they had become this bad. At one point, they were kind of sweet, but I can see that teenage years have brought out a different side in Eliza. She's never reminded me more of her own mother than at this point.

These two might be kids, and they might be my half sisters, but no one is going to talk shit about Ariel in front of me, and I'm not allowing anyone to be disrespectful in my own house.

"Eliza, I'm not going to allow any rudeness toward me and Ariel in my house, so if you don't have anything nice to say, you can go wait in the car," I tell her, then look to my dad, daring him to argue with me. "Or next time, feel free to just stay with your mom."

I've had it.

I don't even care.

"Dad?" she asks, pouting. "You said we'd have fun coming here." She's a little brat, and I don't know how he can deal with this on a daily basis. I feel bad—she's only a kid, after all—but wow.

"Why don't you come and hold Mila? You love babies, remember?" he says, ignoring her complaints.

"No thanks," she grumbles, sighing. "Mom said she's not really related to me anyway, so it doesn't matter."

Ariel, who I think is suddenly feeling a little protective, picks up Mila and cradles her. I think I'm actually speechless, because I have nothing to say right now. They are only kids at the end of the day, but I can't believe how rude Eliza is, and how Dad tolerates it. My mom never would have. We never would have dared to be so rude to anyone, never mind an adult.

"Well, this has been great," Ariel announces, wincing at the lie. "I can see why we only see each other once a year or so."

Probably going to be even less than that after this.

"Why don't you come alone next time, Dad?" I suggest, but then Lucy comes and sits next to me.

"I think Mila is a pretty name," she says. "There's a girl in my class named Mila, and all the boys like her."

My lip twitches at that. Lucy must be about twelve now, but she has a younger vibe about her. "Well, let's hope that's not the case for this Mila, because then Ariel and I will have to put her in an all-girls school."

"Probably a good idea. Boys are trouble," she says, nodding. "Dad said you got a dog. Where is he?"

I let Shadow in, and he steals the hearts of not just Lucy, but Eliza, too. We spend the next hour together, and when they leave, I feel a little better about it than when they first walked in.

And when Ariel opens her present from Dad and inside is a photo album of all her baby photos, an engraved gold chain for Mila and a check for five thousand dollars to start off Mila's savings account, I know that there is a good side to him.

Somewhere in there is the dad who used to come home and kiss us and tuck us in. The dad who made good choices.

And that's something I'm going to hold on to.

Chapter Thirty-Two

Shadow with me, I head to the clubhouse and find the men sitting outside, chatting. I'm about to leave, not wanting to interrupt, when Renny sees me.

"Hey, where are you going?" he calls out, coming over to me.

"You guys look busy," I explain, letting him lead me out there with them. "Hello, everyone." I glance down on the table and see photos of different people lying there, photos from surveillance footage. "What's all this?"

"We've been keeping an eye on all the members of the Killers MC who aren't in prison," Renny explains, sitting down and pulling me onto his lap.

"We wanted to make sure no one was coming for us," Temper adds, leaning back and studying the photos. "We've got eyes everywhere."

One of the pictures captures my attention, so I reach out and pick it up. "Who is this?"

"Why?" Temper asks, glancing between Renny and me. "Have you seen her before?"

I nod. "She has come to my house twice now, saying she lost her dog. She didn't come inside or anything. Ariel spoke to her once and then I spoke to her at the door. Both times she came by for a few short minutes and then left."

"Fuck," Renny mutters under his breath. "This is Skylar's mom, Georgia, the lady we were talking about before. She might look all *Little House on the Prairie*, but she's dangerous and not to be underestimated."

Fear fills me. I got no weird vibes from this woman—she appeared friendly and genuinely concerned about her dog. I'm a person who generally is good at judging someone's character. She had me completely fooled, and I would have been comfortable inviting her in for coffee or something without thinking about it.

My mind is blown right now, and I'm completely speechless. Why did she come to my house? I have to wonder how I factor into her plans here.

"What is she playing at?" Renny asks Temper, holding on to me tighter.

"I think she was trying to get Izzy to trust her," Saint adds, jaw tight. "She looks so sweet that no one would think she's a threat. Maybe she wants more information about something, because she's probably already got some plan up her sleeve."

"I thought she was out of this lifestyle," Dee comments, crossing his arms over his chest. "Yet she's showing up every fucking place we are, first at the mayor's speech and now here. Do I have to go back there? Because that place is a hole. I'm not cut out for the country life."

"She's probably still here," Temper says, turning to Saint. "Keep an eye on Skylar at all times."

"Already on it," Saint says, typing on his phone.

"I can't believe she came to your house," Renny says, looking into my eyes. "Next time tell me if anyone you don't know comes around, okay? I know you wouldn't have thought twice about this, especially a little older lady looking for her dog, but from now on even if it seems like nothing, just let me know."

"I will," I promise.

"Just when we think we can relax a little, we're back on alert thanks to the she-devil," Temper groans, scrubbing his hands down his face.

He looks tired and frustrated, and like he is in desperate need of a long holiday.

"I think I'm going to need to hear this story," I tell Renny, cuddling up to him. "Why is this woman so dangerous?"

Renny tells me the quick version about the story behind Georgia and Skylar. My jaw drops with several plot twists, and by the end of it, I have even more respect for Skylar, if that's possible.

"Holy shit." This woman sounds like the devil incarnate. She's clearly very intelligent, manipulative and a sociopath, and I can see now why it would be a stupid decision to not be wary of her.

"Now that Hammer is gone, though, you'd think her need for revenge would be satisfied," I say to the group.

"We thought so," Saint agrees, nodding. "But at the end of the day, who knows what goes through her mind? She hates the fact that her daughter sits here, not there with her, and that Skylar is loved and protected by the club. She's twisted. And I know she's Skylar's mother and all, but I'd feel a hell of a lot better if she was six feet under."

I can't imagine how Skylar must feel. At the end of the day, that's her mom, and you only get one of those.

The men make a plan to track Georgia and make sure they know where she is at all times. Security is to remain on a high level, and everyone is not to put their guard down.

I think in some ways, though, it's always going to need to be like this.

Because when the guard is down, bad shit happens.

Epilogue

"Hey," I say as Trade steps into the clubhouse with Ariel and Mila at his side. The two of them have been taking things extremely slow, but I think it's safe to say that they are dating. He's at our place almost as much as Renny, especially when his kids are at school, like today, and I like having him around. He's so sweet to my sister and my niece, so what more could I ask for? "How was the zoo?"

"Good," Ariel replies, smiling down at her daughter. "I think we enjoyed it more than Mila, who slept through most of it, but it was a beautiful day out."

"You going to watch this movie with us?" Renny asks them, glancing down at his phone.

"Yeah, we got the message," Ariel replies, wrinkling her nose. "Who knew a whole MC would get together to watch a superhero movie."

"Secret nerds," I say, patting the spot next to me. "I brought snacks, though, so I know it's going to be a good time."

"Dee is bringing beer," Renny adds, grinning at Trade. "And Temper is ordering pizza as we speak."

"No wonder you guys have these giant couches," Ariel

muses, while Trade picks up Mila, who starts to fuss as she wakes.

Sky steps into the room, smiling at us all. "Oh good, I'm not the only one who's early." Her eyes widen as she spots Mila. "Trade, let me hold her. You hog her."

Trade holds Mila closer to his chest. "I do not."

"Someone needs to have another baby so we're not all fighting over mine," Ariel adds, glancing between me and Sky. "Come on, one of you take one for the team."

"Shotgun not," Sky calls out at the same time I shake my head.

The rest of the men arrive, and we all pile into the lounge room together.

I love moments like these, moments when we're nothing but a normal family.

When Renny whispers into my ear that he has a surprise for me, and leads me away from everyone, I have to wonder what the hell he's up to.

"Where are you taking me?" I ask Renny, so tempted to remove the blindfold covering my eyes.

"We're almost there," he promises, carrying me in his arms when my blind walking is taking too long.

Apparently we're both extremely impatient today. I don't know what surprise he has for me up his sleeve, but I'm excited for it. Life has been nothing short of amazing being with Renny, letting him in and truly trusting him. I never thought I'd feel for someone the way I do for him, the love, respect and loyalty he gives me on a daily basis is more than I ever thought I'd have.

When the blindfold comes off, we're at his park, standing in the middle of a circle filled with red roses.

"When did you do this?" I ask, eyes widening as I do a full spin. "It's beautiful, Renny."

My jaw drops open as I see him drop to his knee.

"Izzy, I love you more than anything or anyone in this world, and I want to give you everything. You deserve a proper proposal, engagement and wedding, and I really wanted sober me to pick the ring this time…"

I laugh at that.

"Will you marry me?" he asks, opening the black box to show me the most beautiful pear-shaped halo ring I have ever seen. "For the second time?"

"Yes," I say to him, tears of happiness dripping down my cheeks. "Yes, of course I will."

He slides the ring on my finger, and it fits perfectly, just like the last one did.

Then he stands and kisses me, a long, sweet kiss filled with love and promises.

Staring down at my new ring, I can't believe what the world has handed me in the last year.

One thing I know for sure though, I'm in love with a Knight.

And drunk me knew back then what sober me knows now.

Renegade was meant to be my husband.

* * * * *

*Reviews are an invaluable tool when it comes to
spreading the word about great reads.
Please consider leaving an honest review for this
or any of Carina Press's other titles that you've read
on your favorite retailer or review site.*

*Stay tuned for the next book in the
Knights of Fury MC series,*
Temper,
coming April 2020!

*For more information on books
by Chantal Fernando,
please visit her website at
www.authorchantalfernando.com.*

Acknowledgments

A big thank-you to Carina Press for working with me on the Knights of Fury MC series!

Thank you to Kimberly Brower, my amazing agent, for having my back in all things.

Natalie Ram—I miss you, bestie! It's hard doing life without you, but I know you are just a call away. I love you. Thank you for always reading my work and supporting me, even though I know how busy you are.

Amo Jones—Thank you for always being there when I need someone to talk to, for the badass writing sprints and for encouraging me to be the best writer I can be. You just get me, and finding someone that does that is so rare. I love you, wifey.

Brenda Travers—Thank you so much for all that you do to help promote me. I am so grateful. You go above and beyond and I appreciate you so much.

Ari—You are one of the best souls I have ever met. You are kind, generous, and I'm so lucky to have you in my life. Thank you for always caring about me. I love you!

Tenielle—Baby sister, I don't know where I'd be without you. Thanks for all you do for me and the boys, we all adore you and appreciate you. I might be older, but you inspire me every day. When I grow up, I want to be like you.

Christian—Thank you for always being there for me, and for accepting me just the way I am. I always tell you how lucky you are, but the truth is I'm pretty damn lucky myself. I appreciate all you do for me and the boys. I love you.

To my three sons, my biggest supporters, thank you for being so understanding, loving and helpful. I'm so proud of the men you are all slowly becoming, and I love you all so very much. I hope that watching me work hard every day and following my dreams inspires you all to do the same. Nothing makes me happier than being your mama.

And to my readers, thank you for loving my words. I hope this book is no exception.

About the Author

New York Times, Amazon and USA Today bestselling author Chantal Fernando is thirty-two years old and lives in Western Australia.

Lover of all things romance, Chantal is the author of the bestselling books *Dragon's Lair*, *Maybe This Time* and many more.

When not reading, writing or daydreaming she can be found enjoying life with her three sons and family.

"I'll have a cappuccino, please," a man orders. I nod and write it down so I don't forget. One would think I'd be able to remember one drink without problems, but apparently with me and my usual daydreaming, that's not the case. My head is habitually in the clouds, and sometimes I'm not paying attention even when I think I am.

"No problem," I tell him, smiling. "Anything else?"

He shakes his head.

"Won't be long, sir," I say as I move away and head back behind the counter.

I never thought I'd be working at a café full time at twenty-one, but here I am. I took a gap year after high school, which turned into three, and I don't know, I thought at this age I'd be living a little more. Maybe traveling and seeing the world, with a degree behind me. Experiencing life. Instead I'm serving coffee, living with a friend and barely making ends meet. My brother Brooks moved back to the city at the first opportunity, so I'm the only sibling who is still out here in the country, isolated from the rest. But at least my mom is still here. She lives with her new husband, and we catch up once a week or so.

"Sky, can you cover my shift tomorrow?" asks Max,

my roommate and coworker, blue eyes pleading. "I know it's your only day off, but I have an audition, and I need to be there."

Max is trying to make it big with his band, and I try to help him out when I can so he doesn't lose his job. He is extremely talented, and I have no doubt that they are going to make it—they just need to get their big break.

I was really looking forward to having my day off, but I can't let him miss this. It's not like I had any great plans, other than sitting on my couch. "Yeah, no problem," I tell him, sighing. "Just remember me when you make it big."

"You know I will," he says, leaning forward and kissing my hair. He steps back and looks above me, spreading his palms out, as if imaging his future. "I'll write a song about you. Sky O'Connor, the only one who had my back *before* I was a millionaire."

"I'll be waiting for it," I reply with a smile, finishing up the cappuccino and taking it over to the customer. I spend the next five hours doing much the same, until it's time for me to head home. I get on my bicycle and ride the fifteen minutes it takes to get to my house, with my red ponytail billowing behind me. Max passes me in his car, his honk scaring the shit out of me. They must have let him finish work early, because I know he wasn't meant to go home for another few hours.

"Race you home!" he calls out, and I roll my eyes at him, but start to pedal faster. There's a shortcut I take that actually makes this a fair race, because even in his car, Max has to go around the longer way. I whizz around a lady walking her dogs, then take the sharp turn to the right, rushing toward our house.

When I get there seconds before him, I jump off my bike and do a little happy dance, shaking my booty and flashing him a smug look. "Ha! You lose! Nice try, though, Max."

He gets out of his car and shakes his head at me, laughing. "Whatever, I let you win!"

I cross my arms and narrow my eyes. "You're such a bad loser."

"You're such a bad winner," he grumbles, grabbing the mail before brushing past me to the door. "I hope no one is dropping in tonight so I can run around naked and drink milk from the carton." His friends have a habit of dropping by unexpectedly, and I've somehow gotten used to it.

I wince at that vision. "Umm, hello? Even if no one else is there, I am. And I'd rather not see you naked. Again."

We've been in our apartment for about a year, and in that time we've both caught each other in some pretty compromising positions. I went from growing up surrounded by boys to living with one. Platonically. When I was advertising for a roommate to split the rent, I was hoping a nice woman might come along, but nope. Just an up-and-coming rock star waiting for his big break.

I'm just destined to be surrounded by men I have only platonic feelings for.

"Why not? I look good naked," he brags, unlocking the door and gesturing for me to enter. "Ladies first. But wait, you aren't a lady, so…"

He runs in first and I throw my handbag at him. "You're such a jerk! This is why you're single!"

"I'm single because I'm a player!" the idiot calls back to me, and I can't help but laugh at him. Never a dull moment when Max is around, that's for damn sure. He's like the sixth brother I sure as hell never wanted but got stuck with anyway.

I close the door and head straight for the kitchen, grabbing my bag on the way and placing it down. Picking up the bunch of letters Max threw on the counter, I go through them and pull out the ones for me, walking with them into my bedroom.

"More bills," I grumble, ripping them open. When I come to the last letter, though, it doesn't look like a bill. It's addressed to me in neat handwriting I don't recognize. I open it with caution.

As I read the first line, my heart stops.

Dear Skylar,

Five years. That's a long time to go without talking to somebody, especially someone who was such a huge part of your life. I hope you are well. I don't even know why I'm writing to you, when you're the last person I'd want to know where I am. But you're also the first person who came to mind when they said I could write snail mail. I can't even remember when I wrote something this long. I think maybe it was on your sixteenth birthday when I wrote out the lyrics to your favorite song in your card. Seems like a lifetime ago.

The clubhouse was never the same after you left.

Neither was I.

Saint

Saint.

Saint wrote me a letter. I double-check the envelope, looking at the return address for the first time, and my eyes grow wide.

Saint, my first ever crush, wrote me a letter.

From prison.

"What have you done?" I whisper to myself, reading the letter once more from the top.

"What's that?" Max asks, as he steps into the doorway of my bedroom.

"Nothing," I say quickly, folding up the letter. I left my heart back in the Knights of Fury clubhouse, with Hammer and Saint, and there hasn't been a day that's gone by that I don't think of them. I was never told what exactly happened that night, other than that Mom and Hammer were done with each other and we needed to get away so we were safe. After we left the clubhouse that night, we drove to our house and she had me and my brother Brooks pack everything. We left a day later and never returned.

Neither Hammer nor Saint have ever reached out to me, until right now.

It's not like it's a surprise for one of the bikers to land themselves in prison, but the thought of Saint being there physically hurts me. It means the world to me to hear from him, but at the same time I do feel a little resentful that it took him being locked up to reach out to me. And another thing… I wonder how he knew where I live. Has he known where I've been this entire time?

I need answers.

"Just more bills," I lie, flashing Max a forced smile, wanting to keep Saint to myself. He rolls his eyes and walks away. I get up to shut my door and walk over to my desk to pull out some paper and a pen from my top drawer. I sit down and start to write.

Saint,
I'm sorry to hear from you under these circumstances. Are you okay? If there is anything I can do for you, please let me know. You're right, five years is a long time. I didn't know if I'd ever speak to you again, but I have thought about you often.
   How is Dad?

I pause, then scrub out the word *Dad*, replacing it with *Hammer*.

> *How is Hammer?*
> *He always said I would do great things, far away from the MC, and I guess he was half right. I'm farther away, but I don't know about the doing great things part. I've put college on hold and am just... living.*
> *I guess in prison you'd be doing exactly the same, just living, pushing through to get to the next day.*
> *But things will get better, right?*
> *How much time do you have? I hate the thought of you behind bars, and I hope that you won't be in there for too long. I'm here if you need me, and even though it's probably not much, it's all I can offer right now.*
> *And how did you get my address?*
> *Hang in there, Saint.*
> Love, Sky
> P.S. I still have that sixteenth birthday card.

Don't miss
Saint *by Chantal Fernando,*
available now wherever
Carina Press ebooks are sold.
www.CarinaPress.com